*"I don't know what you look like
But I know that you're there ..."*

I'm singing out my song with raw emotion. I'm
cutting a demo—in a Record Your Own Voice
booth in the Hoboken train station. What else
can I do? Somebody stole my tape recorder with
a tape of my songs in it—and I got a meeting
with an important agent this afternoon. It's a
bad break but I won't let it hold me back.

*"Sometimes I feel your stare,
You'll be the right one."*

Suddenly, there she is! Standing in front of one
of those machines where you stamp your name
on a coin. A beautiful girl with long, silky light
brown hair and huge eyes. She feels my stare,
turns, and meets my eyes. I smile. She smiles
back. I sing the rest of my song to her and she
likes it! Then, I bow my head, look up . . . and
she's gone! I search the whole train station. She's
nowhere in sight. I've got to find her. I have this
feeling, she's the right one.

Voices

A NOVEL
BY
JOHN HERZFELD

WARNER BOOKS

A Warner Communications Company

WARNER BOOKS EDITION

ISBN 0-446-89779-5

Warner Books, Inc.,
75 Rockefeller Plaza,
New York, N.Y. 10019

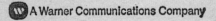 A Warner Communications Company

Printed in the United States of America

Not associated with Warner Press, Inc.,
of Anderson, Indiana

First Printing: February, 1979

10 9 8 7 6 5 4 3 2 1

THIS BOOK IS DEDICATED TO GAMBLERS . . .

NOT THE ONES WHO BET ON TABLES—
BUT THE ONES WHO BET ON PEOPLE.

My name is Drew Rothman, I'm twenty-nine years old. I been around a lot. I used to work in a brewery, now I work for my father's dry cleaners.

I'm a singer.

CHAPTER ONE

ALL OF US COME DOWN THE STAIRS, ONE AFTER another. A singer, a gambler, a tailor, and a wild kid.

We're the Rothmans.

My father Frank's the gambler. He runs the dry cleaning store he inherited from Nathan, his father, the tailor. Frank can't stop gambling, which is the reason Nate never gets off his back.

But this morning, it's my father, Frank, who's on *my* back.

"I know what's botherin' you," he says. "It's not just that somebody stole your tape recorder."

"Nothin's botherin' me," I tell him, opening the front door of our apartment as we walk outside into the cold.

"You need one special woman in your life," he says, turning up his collar. It's winter and the wind from the Hudson River makes the cold colder. "You see a different one every month. You're twenty-nine years old. I married your mother when I was nineteen. What you're lookin' for is an unmarked page."

"I'm not lookin' for anything," I say, turning around to watch Raymond, my fifteen-year-old brother, come out of the building. Raymond's pulling on his coat. Nathan follows behind him.

"Where're your books?" Nathan asks Raymond. "How come ya didn't bring home any books last night?"

"I finished all my homework in study hall yesterday," Raymond says, jamming the last piece of a cold Sara Lee brownie into his mouth, his breakfast.

"I heard ya talkin' on the phone about a big test today. What was that all about?"

"What test?"

"Raymond!"

"It's an oral test! You can't prepare for it. You know it, or you don't!"

As we cut through Elysian Park, which we always do on our way to work, my father keeps at me.

"A girl swears, it bothers you. If she's not wearing a bra, you think she's been with every guy in town."

"I'm not lookin' for anybody," I tell him, taking my lucky silver dollar out of my pocket. I unconsciously rotate it around my forefinger, trying to stay calm.

"You're too choosy," he says, looking out over the Hudson across at New York City. "Cinderella don't live in Hoboken."

When we reach the park swings, my father sees Runner Mike. Mike's sitting on a bench reading a racing form. My father hands Mike an odds sheet, which Mike deposits in a folder. This is a regular morning routine.

"Say hi to Mr. Giasullo for me," my father mutters. Mike nods, not looking up.

Raymond, meanwhile, hands Nathan a pen, then slaps a piece of square paper on a book, and pushes it under Nathan's nose.

"Here, sign this. Right here . . ."

"What is this? Take your hand away."

"It's nothin'. You're sayin' it's okay for me to go on a class trip to the zoo."

Nathan grabs the piece of paper from Raymond's hand.

"This is your report card!"

"It is?"

I drop back and peer over Nathan's shoulder.

"Three Ds, a C, and an F?" I say, glaring at Raymond.

My old man joins us. "How can ya fail math?" he says. "You do so well on the odds sheets."

Nathan flares up. "That's why he fails! He's always studyin' your racing sheets instead of doin' his homework! Raymond, I wanna have a meeting with your teacher."

"She don't go for fat men!" Raymond says.

I smack Raymond on the head. "Always the clown."

Frank grabs the card and signs it.

"Alright, look, we'll talk about this after school," he says. Raymond takes off down the street, just missing a cuff on the head from Nathan.

We exit the park and cross the street to the Rothman Dry Cleaners on the corner of Garden and Third.

"Y'know, you'll never find her, Drew," my father says, never a guy to drop a subject once he gets his teeth in.

"Will ya get off my back? I'm lookin' for nobody!"

Angrily, I yank open the door of the dented Volkswagen van parked in front of the shop. It's red and filthy and ROTHMAN CLEANERS is printed on each side, under which is: YOUR BEST BET. On the back it says: LET US TAKE YOU TO THE CLEANERS.

As I do every morning, I remove the parking ticket from under the windshield wiper, and then slide down behind the wheel. Nathan raps on my window; I roll it down.

"Will ya be back for the afternoon deliveries?" he says.

"I should be, yeah," I answer, zipping up my jacket.

I see Raymond heading into the store. "Hey, I wanna talk to you later!"

"I'll check my schedule an' see if I got time," Raymond says.

As I pull out, I shoot the little wiseguy a look.

My old man's not a bad looking guy. He's got a thick crop of hair, a very strong jaw, and he's still in pretty good shape. He's on the dark side—alluring—my mother used to say, and mysterious. I guess there's a lotta mystery in his face. My old man's not the type of guy that you can look at and know what he's thinking. You can be talking about one thing, and then all of a sudden his brow will furrow, and just when you think he's gonna come out with something relevant to what you been talking about, he'll blurt out something entirely from nowhere. His mind's always working ahead of him, if that makes sense.

My grandfather, Nate, on the other hand, is a big man, strong, with a thick neck. He's seventy-two years old and has a heavy Austrian accent. He doesn't look like a tailor. He looks more like an aging longshoreman, which is what he was until he bought the dry cleaning store and learned to sew.

He hated working the docks. He hated the docks almost as much as he hates shaving, which he only does once a week, and for special occasions, which rarely come up. With his little wire-rimmed glasses, his constant white stubble, and his big stomach, he's a sight. But don't get me wrong, I respect him. The man's been through a lot. When he arrived from Austria and went to work loading ships, the dock workers made fun of him because he didn't speak English; and it didn't make it easier him being Jewish, either. But he's got a great sense of humor and that pulled him through and kept him out of a lotta fights. Plus he had a wonderful wife—though I didn't know my grandmother well. She died when I was twelve.

I think the only time Nate enjoyed working on the docks was when he was in the Service. That's right, he worked on the docks during World War I. You see, Hoboken was our country's official port of embarkation for American troops en route to Europe. The first convoy, carrying almost 12,000 officers, enlisted men, nurses and civilians, left Hoboken on June 14, 1917. Each day an average of 3,500 soldiers left the port. My grandfather told me that one day almost 50,000 left, so you can imagine what Hoboken was like during World War I. It was just crazy. But strangely enough, my grandfather always remembers those days fondly. He's a very patriotic guy, and he loves his country. He loves his city, too.

Hoboken was a beautiful island, way back when, made up of trees and green fields separated from the west by deep marshes, and from the east by a river. The first people that lived here were the Leni-Lenape Indians. They used to camp on the island, but they didn't stay for long periods of time. They named the spot Hopoghan Hackingh, which meant land of the tobacco pipes, because they used the green colored serpentine rocks which are all over this area to carve pipes for smoking tobacco.

In about 1609, a navigator on Henry Hudson's ship, the *Half Moon*, told Hudson about the green rock. This happened on their third voyage up the river, which is now called the Hudson, named after guess who. Anyway, the guys on the *Half Moon* were supposedly the first Europeans to see this island, although if you wanna know how I feel, I personally am not even sure Christopher Columbus discovered America. I heard he discovered Jamaica, and it was Americus Vespucci that discovered America. Anyway, a lotta Dutchmen also visited Hoboken during that time, and Peter Stuyvesant, the Dutch governor of Manhattan, which was then called New Amsterdam, bought all the land around Hackensack and the Hudson River from the Indians for about twelve kettles, six guns, a coupla blankets and a half barrel of beer. So you see, Hoboken is a very important cornerstone of this country.

But I guess the guy that probably did the most to put Hoboken on the map was Colonel Stevens. He was an inventor, who was actually the first guy to discover the steam engine. I know everybody learns in school that Robert Fulton was the inventor of the steam engine, but ask anybody from Hoboken and they'll tell you different. Stevens also designed and built the first experimental steam-driven locomotive in America. Anything that had to do with steam he had his hand in. Stevens Institute of Technology, a very famous institute, was named after him, and is a landmark in Hoboken.

As I drive along my delivery route, I can picture the scene in our dry cleaning store. My old man flicks on the lights, and Nathan asks: "What'd ya say to Drew?"

"Nothin'," my father shrugs. He bangs open the cash register and counts the change. "He's just inna bad mood."

"Why don'tcha get off his back for a change, Frank," Nathan says.

"Why don'tcha get off *my* back for a change, huh, Pa?"

Nate doesn't even bother to answer, it's too early to start arguing. He'll have his coffee first. He pads back to the rear of the store, turning on machines and preparing the place for the day's business, or lack of it, which has lately been the case, because service has been going steadily downhill since my mother passed away almost two years ago and my father stopped caring.

Raymond, meanwhile, is over by the Lions' Club gumball machine in the corner of the store.

My brother Raymond is a schemer, a wiseguy, the class clown, and always getting in trouble, which I always gotta bail him out of, because he likes to hang around with tough guys three and four years older than him. We look alike, too. We both got curly hair and the same eyes.

He smacks the glass ball and a free gumball pops out. He pops it in his mouth, smacks the glass ball again, and a blue one comes out. His constantly plotting mind gets an idea. He palms the blue gumball and glances to the rear of the store to see where Nathan is. Nathan's pulling on his tailor's vest, out of hearing distance, so Ray turns to my father.

"Hey, Dad, what about a little game a chance here? If a blue one comes out, I go to the races with you today."

Without looking up, my father says, "Go to school, Raymond . . ."

"C'mon. Hey, It's such a long shot. Y'know how few blues there are in this machine? C'mere. Look."

Very calmly, my father repeats, "Go to school."

"C'mon, Dad, please! Just one chance." He whispers, "I swear Nate'll never know. Drew won't find out. I won't say a word."

He smacks the machine, and a gumball rolls down and bangs against the metal cover. He doesn't lift the cover.

"Okay, look. If this one is blue, you'll let me come. If it's any other color, I'm on my way to school."

My old man shrugs and walks over to the machine. Actually he loves these games. Anything to do with betting, he's ready. The machine is filled with mostly whites, reds, oranges, greens, and there's very few blue ones in it.

"Blue, huh?" my father asks.

Raymond nods. "Blue."

My father nods, and Raymond lifts the cover, palms the gumball, and turns around to Frank. Then he realizes he made a mistake. He's got a gumball in each hand and the old man's staring at the hand he just reached in with.

"G'head. Open the hand."

Raymond bites his lip, angry at himself. He opens his hand, and stares at the white ball. He looks up at the old man.

"Two outta three . . . ?"

CHAPTER TWO

I was born down in Newark at Beth-Israel Hospital. It was a muggy day. My mother always said I was a laughing baby. Whenever I wanted something, I'd laugh—didn't cry much at all. My mother laughed a lot too. As I said before, she passed away close to two years ago. It hit us all hard, but it floored my father and part of him went with her. He worshipped Rachel. She was his dream girl. He woulda given both arms and legs for her. She was tough, she was strong, she was beautiful, she was sensitive, and she loved him like he loved her.

Me, I haven't met mine yet. I been with a lotta girls. Hoboken's not a big town. We moved up here from Newark in '52 when I was four

17

years old. It was a lot nicer place to live in back then. Still, it's not so bad now. I mean Newark's gone way downhill—a lotta other cities in Jersey, too, but Hoboken's held its own. I think it's even improved. A lot more Spanish people here now. More blacks, more just about everything. I like Jersey. A lotta people knock it, they say it's New York's back door, but me, I think you got a great state here. You got industry, beautiful country, big lakes up north, clean beaches down south, and the people are generally friendly. Sure you got the Mafia here, but show me where you don't. . . .

Me, I'm kinda in an angry mood now. See, I had a cassette recording with six songs on it that I recorded with my band. We're called THE NEW JERSEY TURNPIKE. Yesterday, I was down at the luncheonette on Hamilton Street and somebody stole my cassette. Like a fool I left it in my jacket pocket, and hung the jacket on a coat rack. After a nice lunch of homemade soup and meatloaf, I put the coat on, climbed in the van—I was making deliveries—and I reach in my pocket for my lucky silver dollar, and boom, both are gone. Which was very bad timing, because later in the day I was planning to play that tape for an agent I've been wanting to handle me.

At first, I was very angry. I wanted to go out and pick a fight with a tree—until I came to my senses and went down to the Hoboken train

station where they have a Record Your Own
Voice booth. I decided to record just one of my
best songs, so the agent could get the feel of my
voice.

The train station is really beautiful. If
you got a feeling for old things, you'd love it.
The architect who designed it really did an
amazing job. I think his name was something like
Kenneth Murchinson, or Lurkensen, something
like that. Anyway, Ken did an amazing job, and
this place is very stimulating for me. As a matter
of fact, I think Stephen Collins Foster, the song-
writer, lived right around this area when he
wrote "I Dream of Jeannie with the Light Brown
Hair."

Before I step into the booth, I wave to
Valerie, the girl that works the newsstand. We've
known each other since high school, and I think
she's been working part-time at the newsstand
since then.

Valerie and I dated off and on ten years
ago. She was a nice girl, very popular in high
school. She's still a nice girl, just forty pounds
heavier. She married a black mechanic named
Tyrone. Theirs was the first interracial marriage
in Hoboken. And of all the couples I know who
got married right outta high school, they are the
only one still going strong. Good people.

Me, I been coming to the booth since I'm
a kid. That's how I really started getting interested in singing. Everybody in this town always

talks about Frank Sinatra, since he comes from Hoboken, so when I was ten years old, I came down here and cut my first single: "Jailhouse Rock."

I have two hundred and fifty-two recordings in my room. I don't know why I hold on to 'em. Nostalgia, I guess.

The recording booth's on the second balcony overlooking the train station. You can see and hear everything from here. Behind the booth there are some pinball machines and other quarter games to test your skill. Do you wanna know the truth? I never go near these machines. I have never in my life liked the game of pinball. I've tried, but I just can't get a kick out of it. People I know go nuts over the game. Me, I can't find any challenge in standing in front of a machine pushing two flippers, trying to knock a marble into a hole so a light'll light up and you can get another free game to do it all over again. Pool I like to shoot now and again, darts I'm not bad at, but pinball or these other quarter games —never. I don't play.

I close the door to the booth and put the cotton in my ears. I use cotton to block out the noise. Also, it helps me get in the mood. I sing into a big souvenir pencil I bought when I was nine down in Asbury Park. I pretend it's a microphone and it helps. Fantasy is very important. I fantasize all the time . . .

I put three quarters in the machine and shut my eyes. From far away, I hear the announcer's voice . . .

*"Ladies and gentlemen, the
management of the MGM Grand Hotel
in Las Vegas is proud to bring you,
straight from a standing-room-only
tour of record-breaking engagements,
the one, the only, the electric, the
magical Mr. Velvet Throat himself, the
idol of millions the world over,
JERSEY DREW ROTHMAN!"*

I hear the applause and the women scream. I see myself out on that wide, elevated stage—white suit, blue spread-collar shirt. I'm tan, looking great, and the throat's in perfect condition. A few chords from the piano and I begin to sing. I wrote the song myself.

I just started writing songs last year. Well, that's not totally true, I've been at it a few years, but until last year I didn't think I had anything good enough to put down on paper. My song writing improved when I started getting decent at the piano. I bought a used upright three years ago. Up until then I didn't play an instrument, I just sang . . . and not professionally either, and not wholeheartedly, either. I was working in a brewery in Secaucus. Then finally one day I quit the job and went at my singing seriously. I saw life passing me by and me accomplishing nothing. Now I don't fear failure. You only live once. I'm giving the singing my best shot. I'm gonna make it or die trying.

I wrote this song by humming it into a tape recorder. I can't read or write a note of music, I just hum the tune, then my friend Petey, the drummer in my band, comes over and writes it on paper. We do this, that is when he's not stoned out, which he is a lotta the time. Me, I don't smoke grass. I like to stay in control of things. Maybe I am a little too tight, maybe I don't relax enough, which is what Mark, the guitarist in my band says, but that's the way I am. Anyway, then me and Petey, who's black, and by the way's related to Valerie's Tyrone—I told you this city was a small place—get together with the rest of the band and arrange it.

This song is very personal. As I said before, I been with a lotta girls, but I still haven't met the right one. That's what the song's about. Coincidentally, it's called "You'll Be the Right One". The lyrics, maybe they're not Grammy material, but they're me. I sing:

> *I don't know what you look like*
> *But I know that you're there*
> *Sometimes I feel your stare*
> *You'll be the right one . . .*

With a wave of my hand, I pull in a piano.

> *Still livin' alone*
> *And wonderin' why*
> *Time just keeps flyin' by*
> *You'll be the right one . . .*

Now I pull in the guitar and drums. My eyes are closed and I can hear the music. The bass joins us too, as I break into the chorus:

22

But I know that you're out there so
      I'm waitin' ...
Takin' a break from one-night stands
      'cause I awaken,
The next mornin' like a tunnel inside
(I feel so hollow)
I'm an angry train that rides right on by
(I feel so hollow)
The next morning like a tunnel
      inside ...

As I sing out the third verse, I reach into the air and pull in a hot saxophone.

The city's so crowded
And the parks overflow
With couples y'know
Makes me jealous.

Friends my own age
Droppin' children at school
I'm a fire fulla fuel
Burnin' nowhere.

But I know that you're out there
So I'm waitin' ...

Then I open my eyes, and oh my God! There *she* is. Standing down on the lower level of the train station. A beautiful girl looking up at me. She's standing in front of one a those machines, where you pull down the lever and stamp your name on a Western coin.

I smile. She smiles. I rock out and cut loose with my ballad. I don't know what I look like, with the cotton sticking outta my ears and singing into this big pencil, but she stays with me and I sing the song *to her*. I don't even notice when I run out of time and the record's not recording anymore. When the song's over, I bow my head. My heart's pounding and I sweat right through my shirt.

Then I lift my head up and she's gone ! ! !

I grab my record and almost rip the door off the booth. I speed down the stairs, taking three at a time, and jump the last six. I look all over the station. Valerie shouts something at me but I don't hear. I run out to the Tubes, the subway that goes to New York under the Hudson River, but she's nowhere in sight. I hurry over to the lead car of a train that's pulling out. I look in every car as they pass me, but she's not in any of them. I trot back through the station and out the front door.

She's disappeared! She's nowhere!

Then I remember the coin machine. She was standing in front of it. I go back inside the station and run to the machine.

I cross my fingers, grab a holda the lever, and then I pull it down. Would you believe it, a coin comes out with a name stamped on it . . .

ROSEMARIE LEMON

CHAPTER THREE

IT'S LATER IN THE DAY AND I'M BEHIND THE WHEEL of the cleaning van, driving down the New Jersey Turnpike on my way into Newark. That's where the agent's office is. On Broad and Market. Broad Street is the main avenue in Newark. It runs east and west, from one end of the city to the other. It's like a New Jersey version of Broadway. As a teenager, I came down here a lot because the new movies would open in Newark first. I lived in movie theaters as a kid. I love pictures. Especially the musicals, and especially ones Frank Sinatra was in. I don't know him, I never met him, but I feel kind of a comradeship with him. Why is obvious. As a matter a fact he sang his first important solo concert at the Mosque Theater in Newark, which is now called the Symphony Hall, but now they got mostly rock concerts.

I park the van right in front of the agent's building. I'm in a red, no-parking zone, but I slip the ticket under the windshield. It always works for me. Like my father I love to take chances. But I don't bet anymore because I don't have the money to lose. I mean, I grew up playing poker. I learned it from my father who used to hold games in the living room every Thursday night until he started losing so heavily my mother made him give it up. Now he blows all his money at the track. And he's drinking too much, and getting a little paunch, and for my father that's really something 'cause he was always very proud of his body. I got that from him. I work out with weights. I figure I'm only gonna go through life once so why not go through it as physically fit as possible. I don't feel good if my body's not in shape and I don't sing good if I don't feel good. In high school, I broke my right arm in a fight with Pinky De Soto, and couldn't really exercise for three and a half months till I got the cast off. Well, it really affected me. I never felt right, and a funny thing started to happen which helped me learn something important about myself. Not feeling good physically, I started not feeling so good about myself mentally, which resulted in my not feeling so good about other people. Before I knew it, I became a lousy grouch. Which led me to a brilliant conclusion: If you don't like yourself it's hard to like other people. Maybe it's not such a brilliant conclusion, but it has helped shape my philosophy on life. Like yourself, do what you want to do, and you'll be a lot happier.

As I lock the van, I'm finishing up an apple, which I started less than a minute before. I always eat too fast but I never get indigestion. As a matter of fact, I've never had indigestion in my whole life. I guess I'm lucky.

Anyway, as I step up to the building, I spot a sewer across the street, and being a very superstitious guy, I do what I always do. I wind back with the apple core and in my mind I say to myself if it goes in, the agent will sign me. I heave it, it bounces off the sewer grill, rebounds off the curb and comes to rest just inches away from the opening . . .

I'd like to kill that sewer, I'm thinking to myself as I enter the building. But just as I reach the elevator I shrug it off. That one didn't count, I say to myself.

To be quite honest, when I was a kid I had a heavy fear of elevators. Not all elevators, just ones like I'm about to get in. See, this building is very old and this elevator, I'm sure, is one of the first of its kind. It's an antique. First you have to open this heavy door, then you pull the old gate to one side and step in.

I punch the third floor button and it takes at least a minute for the elevator to even start to move. When I was eight, I spent the entire night in the elevator of my grandfather's building. I had a big blowout with my old man when he accused me of stealing golf clubs from W.T. Grant's. I had given them to him for his birthday after reading an article in *Sports Illustrated* that said golf was the new sport of the leisure class and the perfect activity for the up-and-coming businessman. At that time the dry cleaning business was going terrific, thanks to him, so I went out and got the clubs: a driver, an iron, and a putter. From the magazine article it looked like that's all you needed.

How I got 'em was easy. It was a slow Monday afternoon as I entered Grant's on the bottom floor and headed for the sports department. I walked into the store dragging my right leg, pretending it was wooden. I had a terrible limp. Of course, all the sales people saw me and, though I didn't look at them, I could tell they were feeling sorry for me. As I limped toward the sporting goods, a kindly salesman asked if I needed any help. I said no thanks and he left me alone, not wanting to patronize me. Exactly what I wanted...

After making sure no one was watching, I stuck a driver down my pants leg, deposited two Spaulding golf balls in my underwear (makes sense, right?), and limped out of the store.

I hid the club and balls across the street in the woods, then reentered the store from another entrance. The next trip, I brought out a nine iron and two balls, and on the last, I got the putter and two more balls.

Then I slipped into Woolworth's, copped some wrapping paper and Scotch tape, and that night when my father got home from work, I presented my present, accompanied by a large smile.

He and my mother exchanged looks—and then dead silence. They assumed I stole the clubs. I swore I didn't, but they didn't believe me and I was very hurt. So I ran across town to get some sympathy from my grandparents. They didn't know I was coming, so when I got stuck in the elevator, they didn't know it. My father and mother thought I had run away from home. No one knew where I was, so I spent the entire night in the elevator. That was the first time I got stuck in an elevator. Believe it or not, I been stuck in eight elevators. So you see, it's not like I'm a claustrophobic, it's just that I have bad luck with elevators.

I woulda taken the stairs, but that's what I did the first time I came to see this agent and I ended up getting locked in the stairwell. It's ridiculous, you can get in these stairwells, but you can't get out. I don't know what happens in case of fire. You come leaping down the stairs and *boom*, you're locked in. Someone I'm sure has an explanation for it. I'd love to meet the man and hear it.

What seems like an hour later, the elevator stops at the third floor and I step out quickly. The green hallway is narrow and the paint is peeling off the ceiling. But this agent, Montrose Meier, used to be very famous and has a lot of connections.

I have my record in my hand as I open the door to his office. His secretary, Mildred,

29

who looks about ninety, raises her head and gives me a very unwelcome look. I don't give her a chance to tell me to leave.

"I know Mr. Meier's too busy to drop in at the club where I work, so all I want's two minutes of his life. Is that too much to ask, Mildred? Is two minutes too much?"

I hear Meier yell from the inner office. "Who is it?"

He's gotta voice that always sounds like he's shouting through a tunnel. Right at that moment, I decide I'm just gonna walk into his office.

Mildred yells, "You can't go in there."

Meier's sitting behind his cluttered desk, his white hair is parted down the middle, and autographed photos of stars of yesterday decorate his walls. He's got Vic Damone, Eddie Fisher, Perry Como, a big one of Frank, plus a lot of guys I never heard of. He's wearing the same black and brown pinstripe suit he was wearing not the last time, but the time before last that I was here. I don't give him a chance to throw me out either.

"All I want's for you to listen to this— say no, an' I'm out the door."

Mildred grabs my arm and looks apologetically at Mr. Meier.

"I'm sorry, Mr. Meier."

I put my record right down on Meier's desk. "Please, all I want you to do is listen to this."

He examines the record's label which reads, "Record Your Own Voice."

He looks up at me. "This is a joke?"

"I had a cassette recorder, but somebody stole it, along with all my good tapes. My name is Drew Rothman and I been here a hundred times . . . I'm a singer."

He stands up, measures me, and realizes that this time I'm not leaving until he hears me.

"Alright, you got two minutes."

He walks over to a portable record player on the windowsill. As he puts the record on the turntable, I say, "Ya gotta take into account it's a cheap recording."

He turns around and gives me this look. Then he nods to the secretary and she leaves. As he places the needle on the record he looks at his watch.

My voice comes out of the little speaker, *a capella*. It's funny, but I'm surprised to hear myself singing alone. I forgot that the music that I was hearing as I was singing was all in my head. My voice does not sound great either. Plus you can hear one of the pinball machines in the background. Some kid is kicking it and cursing. I had the cotton in my ears and didn't hear it. Anyway, the record's only playing ten seconds when Mildred buzzes him over the intercom.

Meier pushes the button.

"Yeah . . ."

"Mr. Debbs from Tiny's Hideaway."

Meier grins. "Oh yeah, put him on."

"Ernie, how are you? 'Course I got comics. . . . Dirty, are you kiddin'? Ever hear of Nicky Bluenose? He's been packin' 'em in at the Cinnamon Shoe." Meier chuckles to himself.

"Why, he's so funny, Ernie, he's so funny, last night a guy in the first row was laughin' so hard he had a seizure an' Nicky's such a trouper, he didn't even stop the show when the rescue squad arrived."

Meier winks at me like I'm supposed to think that's funny.

"Hey Ernie, I'll send you a tape of his stuff right away . . . Hey, how's you wonderful wife? . . . Great! . . . How's your girlfriend?"

He winks at me again. I'm getting very tense. He's not hearing a word of my music.

"Terrific Ernie . . . I'll talk to you, when? Monday? Beautiful. Till then Ernest . . ."

He hangs up the phone just as "You'll Be the Right One" is finishing.

"Great, kid, really liked the voice. Terrific. Stick with it."

I shift in my seat and try and stay cool.

"How could ya hear it?"

"Hey," he answers, "I always do two things at once. And what I think is just like I said, stick with it. You gotta good sound. I dig you."

I'm very surprised. I lean back in my chair. Maybe he *can* do two things at once! I start to feel a little bit happy.

"Oh, wow, thanks," I say.

He nods, relights his cigar, and leans back in his chair.

"But personally I'm not interested 'cause I only handle stars."

For some reason I stand up fast.

"Sit down, sit down. Take a look at this guy."

I sit down. He picks up off his desk an 8x10 photo of a young muscleman my age, posing with a microphone in his hand. . . . A typical Newark greaseball.

He holds up the 8x10. "Stars—like Johnny Newark—that's who I handle."

He looks proudly at the picture. Maybe, I think to myself, Johnny Newark's his nephew.

"This week Johnny's playin' the Red Room at the Ramada Inn. Saturday, he sings at the fiftieth anniversary party of the American Can Company. He was last year's Mister Transit Authority. He's on the rise. What's your name? Drew? Drew, how can I put this . . ." He leans forward on his desk, and picks his nose real fast like I'm not supposed to notice.

"I like you, you seem like a nice kid. But you see, I only handle the filet mignon of this business—like Johnny!"

"Johnny's steak and I'm a hamburger. Is that what you're sayin'?"

He smiles.

"Hamburgers are the staple of America. Look at McDonald's!" He picks up a wrapper off his desk, cold cheese sticking to it, then suddenly becomes serious and leans forward. "Hey, you asked for my opinion."

I'm on my feet again and I'm mad. What right does he have to talk to me like this? I walk around his desk.

"I'm not a hamburger," I say, feeling heat on the back of my neck.

He gets outta his chair. He realizes maybe he said the wrong thing.

"Say no, an' I'm out the door—that's what you said," he blusters nervously.

I look at him and decide he's not worth it. He's not worth doing anything that might get me in trouble . . . "Thanks," I tell him, pick up my record, and leave.

I walk outside and suddenly stop. Several yards away is a telephone booth. I reach inside my pocket and pull out the Rosemarie Lemon coin. I try to gauge the distance between myself and the booth. I say to myself: fifteen steps, I find the number, I call her, and we'll have a date. I start walking toward the booth, counting the steps. At twelve, I'm still a good distance from it. I try to get there with three big gigantic steps. I'm still one step away!

Aggravated, I enter the booth. I take these games seriously. I pick the telephone book off the ground and open it to the "L"s. There is only one Lemon, spelled with one "m". It's a doctor, A.W. Lemon. I reach in my pocket and all I have is my new lucky silver dollar, and some bills. But luck is on my side. It's an old phone with the black rubber cord attaching the receiver to the box. I carry a thumbtack for just these emergencies . . .

I stick the thumbtack through the wire and touch the head to the metal on the coin return. A tiny spark and then—instant dial tone! Don't ask me why, but it works. I been doing it since I'm a kid. I learned it at the Cabana Club, which was a ritzy private swim club in Fairlawn. During the summers, when I was a kid, me and my best friend, Pinky (who's no longer a friend —we went different ways in high school after a good fight, the one I broke my right arm in) would hitch over to Fairlawn, it's only fifteen minutes away, and climb over the fence in the back by the tennis courts, change into our bathing suits behind the day camp shacks and then slip into the huge pool when the lifeguard wasn't looking. Almost always we'd get kicked out. One of the three lifeguards would see one of us and we'd hear: "Hey, you two, you don't belong here, you're not members. Out!" We'd be escorted out of the club and warned that next time they'd call the police, which they did a few times, but we'd always run away before the cops got there. For the next week or two, we'd sneak in other clubs.

Anyway, as a result of those summers, I learned to swim great underwater. The thumb-tack free phone call bit I learned one day from a daycamp counselor I met at one of the clubs, who was from Trenton. A girl he dated lived up the street from me.

I dial the number. A woman's voice answers.

"Hello."

I'm hopeful. "Hello, ah, can I speak to Rosemarie, please?"

"Who?"

"Does the doctor have a daughter named Rosemarie,?"

"Rosemarie? The doctor's not even married. What number are you dialing?"

I heave a sigh of disappointment. "The wrong one," I say and hang up.

CHAPTER FOUR

I GOTTA HABIT OF TWIRLING A COIN OVER MY knuckles. I saw Van Heflin do it in a movie once, or maybe it was Van Johnson—I don't know, one of those Vans. He was a gangster on the run, holing up in a small town. One night he's sitting on the stoop talking to some girl he really liked. Or maybe he didn't like her, I don't know, I really can't remember. All I remember about the movie is the coin trick, and that one of the bit players had his toupee on crooked. The toupee stuck in my mind 'cause I went to school with a kid whose hair fell out when he was sixteen. He also wore a toupee, which was always crooked.

I'm back in Hoboken, driving the van down Sixth Street, which is near where we live. As I drive I'm trying to twirl that Rosemarie

Lemon coin across my knuckles. These coins are really big, plus they're too light to really do the trick with, but it's a challenge and I love challenges.

I realize the light's red, and I hit the brakes just in time. I'm lucky, there's a cop standing at the corner. But then I notice he's eating lunch and I see he's a friend of mine. I graduated high school with him. His name is Ronnie and it's amazing he ever became a cop. He and his twin brother, Ricky, were the toughest, meanest, most delinquent kids in the entire school, and both set a record for the most suspensions in one year. They tied each other. They always did everything together. I like Ricky better than Ronnie, but both are semi-friends, which means I'm not their enemy. We were all always in the same division, since junior high. We always went to the same classes together . . .

See, in my high school, Jefferson High, kids were separated into divisions. Meaning they were grouped according to their intelligence. So you went from class to class with the same kids throughout your entire junior-high and high-school experience. There were five divisions. For example, in ninth grade, 9–1 was for college preparatory students. That was not a big division in Hoboken. 9–2 was for B+ students, kids that might possibly get to college; 9–3 was for average students; 9–4 was all male, and consisted of wiseguys and troublemakers, and 9–5 was the retarded class at the end of the hall . . .

The school had unique methods for dealing with the students in my division, 9–4. From ninth grade to senior year, I had gym first thing in the morning. As soon as we got to school, we had homeroom class and then we went straight to gym. Dr. Murray, the principal, figured let the kid get it outta his system as soon as he gets to school and maybe he'll be calmer during the day and not cause as many problems. Using that same philosophy, we had gym again right before school let out—figuring again, let them get it out before they get back on the streets.

Sounds good, right? It never worked. It never worked for a number of reasons. First of all, gym didn't tire anybody out. Gym got you going even more, and the last period gym class would initiate arguments that, as soon as school let out, would be settled over at Vincent's Pond. The best way to describe gym would be to say it was a zoo without bars. The smaller kids dreaded gym like the bubonic plague.

My class was made up of "ethnics"—Italians, Jews, Spanish, and a few blacks. There wasn't a gentile kid in the class. Every kid had hot blood. And during those years, '63 to '66, things were broiling in the City across the river. See, what was happening at that time was that Hoboken was becoming integrated. A lotta Cubans and Puerto Ricans started moving in. Not many blacks, just mostly Latinos. I would say that today Hoboken's half Spanish. Today everybody gets along pretty well, but back then it was not the case.

Back then, Italians hung out with Italians, Jews with Jews, blacks with blacks. Then came the Spanish! Everybody resented them!

So, gym class was one big, ongoing duel with soccer balls used as pistols. Soccer balls? Yes, soccer balls were very instrumental in my upbringing, yet to this day, I've only played the game one time. Our division played it once and then it was quickly abandoned. A sport based on kicking was not a good idea for Division 4.

Gym class went like this. First, we'd line up according to height. Nobody wore matching uniforms, except basically the Jews wore T-shirts, the Italians wore undershirts, the blacks wore ripped shirts, and the Cubans wore no shirts.

After we were lined up, the coach would stroll out. Coach Kapp was German, despised us all, and had as little to do with us as possible. The coach had only one goal in life, which he was not able to keep very secret: to get into the nurse's pants. She was divorced, not that pretty, but a wonderful woman.

Anyway, at the beginning of class he'd walk out into the middle of the floor with three soccer balls under each arm. These balls were used in a game called Battle Ball. It's a very simple game. We were divided in half. Half stepped to one side of the gym, half to the other. The coach always let us duke up our own teams, but since the class was more or less thirty-five percent Italian, twenty-five percent Jewish, twenty percent Cuban, fifteen percent black, and five percent mixed, this never worked and enemies would end up on the same side. Then the coach would walk up the black line that divided the gym, throw the balls in the air and hurry back to his office. The object of the game was to run up to the black line and hit somebody on the other side, anywhere from the head to the toe. If he caught the ball, you were out. If he didn't, he was out. On more than one occasion some guys got knocked out—literally, 'cause those soccer balls were very, very hard.

Needless to say, as soon as the coach closed the door to his office, all hell broke loose! No one paid attention to any rules and soccer balls flew everywhere for fifty minutes straight! On a few other occasions when the coach was feeling particularly frustrated, he would "let us" use basketballs, and even once, footballs, which proved to be his downfall. Fourteen kids ended up in the nurse's office that day, and the coach wasn't invited to return to school the following fall.

That year, 1966, the year I graduated, was the last year the sport was played this way. And the double gym classes were also ended that year. My brother, Raymond, plays Battle Ball a lot, but now only volleyballs are used, and the new coach remains in class during the game.

I guess if I had to single out the most terrifying experience I had in my entire high school career, I'd have to say it was when Michael Scalisi tried to strangle me.

It all started out as a joke, Pinky's joke.

You see, every now and then some of the kids from the retarded class down at the end of the hall were allowed to have gym with us. One of these retarded students was named Michael

Scalisi. Michael resembled a small tree. He was six foot six, weighed about 280 pounds and was solid rock. He always reminded me of that character, Lenny, from *Of Mice and Men*, . . . big, nice, but dimwitted. He never bothered anybody and rarely spoke unless spoken to. A few times I talked to him. As a matter of fact I went outta my way to talk to him 'cause I always wondered what made him tick, and he was really a nice guy. I used to see him walking to school in the morning. I even walked to school with him twice. He just never really had much to say, and when he did, he usually stuttered.

Anyway, Michael never played Battle Ball, he'd just stay on his own, go in the weight room and lift weights. Nobody ever bothered Michael. I mean who's gonna bother a guy that can bench press 350 pounds 40 times, *and* do four sets in less than ten minutes?

One day, Pinky and Donny Blueberry— we called him that because he had this like wart on his forehead that looked like a blueberry— went into the weight room and told Michael that I was going around the gym telling everybody that Michael was so dumb he couldn't pass puberty. It's funny, right? At another time I mighta laughed at that joke. Anyway, after they explained to Michael what puberty was, they led him outta the weight room and pointed across the gym at me where I happened to be laughing at a joke another guy had just told me.

I'll never forget the next coupla minutes. The bell rang, and I was on my way to the locker room when Michael walked over to me, placed

both of his mammoth hands around my neck
and lifted me off the ground! I dangled like a
yo-yo. He just held me straight out in front of
him, squeezing. I started kicking him with all my
might, but he wouldn't let go. I landed some
good shots, even one I thought hit him between
the legs, but his hands did not budge. All I remember is everybody crowding around and even
Pinky trying to pull him off, but he was like a
dog who'd bitten into something and would not
unclench his jaws. Finally, right before I blacked
out, I remember seeing the coach run over and
smash a trash basket over his head.

I was all right. I came to in the nurse's
office. I had nightmares for a coupla weeks, but
otherwise I was okay.

Raymond's in 9–2. If he really wanted to,
he could be in 9–1—he's that bright, when he
wants to be, though he rarely uses his brains at
all. Which is what he was in the process of doing
—not using his brains—when I drove down Hill
Street and spotted him with his gang—the
Gladiators.

The Gladiators are playing a game called
Toll Road, which I invented years ago and which
is not really a game but an excuse for extorting
money from passing motorists. (I started the
gang with Pinkey, who later broke off and
started one of his own, the Warriors.)

It's done like this. A kid about seventeen,
who's probably just got his driver's license, is
cruising with his girlfriend through the streets of
Hoboken. He's from one of the Oranges or from

some upper-middle-class area of New Jersey, 'cause he isn't familiar with the streets—see, a lotta kids come up here and cruise because the city is very scenic right along the river.

All the Gladiators have wooden swords and garbage can tops which they fight each other with in the middle of the street.

So the kid drives down the street and to his surprise he sees this young gang playin' gladiators with each other in the middle of the street. He honks the horn of his brand new Triumph and yells out the window.

"Hey what's going on, what is this?"

Raymond goes right into his wiseguy voice, which is a mixture of W.C. Fields and Jimmy Cagney.

"A toll road, rich boy. One dollar of your daddy's money an' we'll let you go."

The boy looks at his girlfriend, then honks the horn bravely and yells: "Get outta the way, you little maniac!"

Raymond nods to the Gladiators and they surround the car as Raymond places the pointed tip of his wooden sword on the new hood and grins with a devilish gleam in his eye.

"How 'bout a nice long deep scratch right down the center of your hood? Or should I carve your girlfriend's initials in it? What're your initials, honey?"

The driver's date, a cute blonde, looks at her boyfriend.

"Bobby, your father will kill you."

Raymond crosses around to her window.

"I'll bet you're a Judy? . . . No? Carol?

Susan? Whatta ya doin' Saturday night? Dump this lightweight. What's your phone number?"

My brother's talking a mile a minute, having a great time, being the star of the show. Sometimes I think he might grow up to be an actor.

"I'm gonna call the police!" the kid says.

Raymond turns to the other members of the gang and laughs, "Give the kid a dime! They'll clean this area up, the cops will. Ya got till three, Bobby boy—an' since you're causin' me to lose my patience, we're up to two dollars. . . . One—two—"

"Pay them, Bobby. I told you we shouldn't have come down here," the blonde says nervously.

Raymond grins. "Slumming costs these days. . . . Oh, Susie, we'd be great together. Two and nine-tenths . . ." He looks at Bobby. "Two and nine-tenths of nine-tenths . . ."

Bobby angrily fishes out his wallet and Raymond snatches out a five. "Thanks for the tip, Bob."

Bobby reaches for the five-dollar bill, Raymond pulls back and snarls: "Go on, beat it punk."

The Gladiators part, Raymond tips his cap, winks at the girl, and the car speeds off as Raymond shouts:

"Come again, bring friends!"

Then Demetrius, the tallest Gladiator, Raymond's best friend, nudges Raymond and gestures up the street toward me. I yank the van over to the side of the street and climb out. I told

Raymond what I was gonna do to him if I ever caught him playin' this game again. We've had long talks about Toll Roading. It landed me in Juvenile Court, and I want him to avoid my mistakes.

He sees me coming and runs. I take off after him. I chase him through Elysian Park and catch him in an alley on the other side, next to our building.

"Leave me alone!"

"What'd I tell ya I'd do next time I caught ya?"

"If you stick me upside down in a garbage can, I'll gouge your eyes out while ya sleep." He grabs a bottle and smashes off the bottom. "Don't come any closer."

"You turn a broken bottle on your own brother?"

"I'll cut out your song box!"

I rush him. He throws the bottle down, scared. I hoist him over my head and hold him upside down over a garbage can.

"He said he'd cripple me if I didn't pay!"

"Who?"

"Johnny De Soto!"

I return him to his feet, and push him up against the wall.

"You been playin' poker in the boys' room again?"

"Where else am I gonna play?"

"Why are you such a bad kid?"

"I take after you!"

I notice he's wearing a new watch on his wrist.

"Where'd you get that?"

He plays stupid. "What?"

"That!"

"This?"

I tighten my grip around his collar.

"I won it from Danny Feinstein! You're chokin' me! You're chokin' me!"

I loosen my grip a little. "Where'd *he* get it?"

He avoids my eyes. "What do I care? It works. Hey, did that agent sign ya?"

I let him go. I sigh. I start walking home. "No."

He catches up to me.

"Why not? You didn't play your record for him?"

"Yeah. He heard me sing."

"So what happened? The bum heard ya sing. What happened?"

I turn to him. All of a sudden, I'm feeling tired. It's been a long day.

"He don't handle hamburgers . . ."

CHAPTER FIVE

I TOLD YA BEFORE THAT THE GYM CLASS IN MY school was a zoo without bars. Well, a family dinner in the Rothman kitchen is a three-ring circus, minus the rings.

There are no boundaries. Everybody's arguing, grabbing, talking at once. Not a nice atmosphere to eat in, but luckily I don't get indigestion. The apartment itself shows absolutely no sign of a woman. It's sloppy and dusty, and I'm personally very ashamed, but not ashamed enough to clean it myself. Needless to say, I never bring guests home.

You'd probably think that after my mother passed away we would have assigned each other certain tasks to keep the house running in order. Not the case. No one does anything, and sometimes the garbage sits in the kitchen for two days before someone takes it out. Dishes are always overflowing outta the sink, and my grandfather's clothes are everywhere because he sleeps in the living room. When he removes an article of clothing it stays there.

Tonight, dinner consists of pizza, bagels and cream cheese, Wheaties, milk, danishes, gefilte fish, a can of herring which only Nathan slurps at, Pepsi, wine, and a beer for me.

As I sit down, my father turns to me with food in his mouth.

"Hamburgers! What the hell is Raymond talkin' about?"

Before I can answer, Nathan chimes in, "Hey, Drew, I heard a lotta people passed on Frank Sinatra before he got noticed by the right person. Elvis, too. Six agents I heard turned him down before he got discovered by that Chicken Colonel."

"I never heard those stories," I say.

Raymond grabs for the wine; my father slaps his hand. My father turns to me.

"Ahh, that Meier's a scumbag."

Nathan coughs and jabs me. "Your grandfather doesn't lie. Ask your father about the Chicken Colonel story. Don't give up. Ask Frank." He turns to my father. "Didn't ya hear that?"

Frank looks up from his racing form. "Hear what?"

Nathan snatches the form away from my father. "Are you part of this family?"

My father is patient. "Don't do that."

"We're having dinner!"

"Don't bend the form. Just give it back before . . ."

My grandfather doesn't give him a chance to finish. "Can't you figure out how to throw your money away later, after dinner?"

"I'm throwin' my money away, is that what I'm doin'?"

He grabs a wad of cash out of his pocket and dumps it on the pizza.

"Six hundred and forty-four dollars to be exact, I won two days ago."

My grandfather remains unimpressed.

"You set a great example for Raymond."

"This I put away for Raymond's college education. I don't make this kinda money cleaning clothes."

"You would if you ran the business right."

My father sighs and wipes his mouth. "Why didn't I move the family to California after Rachel died?"

"Let's not get into that again, okay? Every night you guys argue over the business. Let's talk about Raymond," I say.

"Let's not and say we did," Raymond quips.

I turn to my father. "He's collectin' tolls again."

My father sets down a piece of pizza, which he's eating intermittently between bites of gefilte fish.

"Alright Raymond, that's it, no more allowance!"

"You took his allowance away last week," I inform my father.

"I did?"

Nathan yells. "What kinda goddamn father are ya? If Raymond was running at Monmouth, you'd know his life history." He snatches the racing form away from my father and tears it into small pieces.

My father glares at him. My grandfather glares back.

"What is this look? Are you supposed to be scaring me, Frankie?"

My father turns to me and Raymond. "It's sad to look at your grandfather and know he's going senile, isn't it?" Suddenly he whirls on Nathan. "Did you know I read in the *Star Ledger* that by the time Raymond goes to college it's gonna cost ten thousand figures?"

"What if I don't wanna go to college?"

"You're goin' to college!"

"That's it, scream at your son!"

"School is a waste of time. I'm gonna be a gambler like you!"

This statement raises the veins in Nathan's neck. "You see what your influence has done!"

My ears are rattling. I stand up fast.

"One night! One night a dinner that doesn't turn into a circus! Can't that be done? Look at this crap! Garbage. I'm not eating it anymore." I fling the pizza into the trash.

Raymond looks up. "We had chicken last night."

"Barbecue, take out. Everything's always take-out."

"Then defrost your own dinner," my father says as he starts to piece together his racing form.

"I'm not eating TV dinners anymore, and neither is Raymond." I throw Raymond's pizza in the trash.

"What are ya doin'?"

"This stuff'll stunt your growth. Ya need protein."

"He's right," Nathan agrees. "Somebody should cook in this house." He tosses his pizza into the garbage.

"Meat and potatoes, that's what we should eat!" I look at Raymond. "What time is it?"

He pushes up his sleeve and checks his new watch. "It's almost seven-thirty. You're gonna be late!"

I grab my coat. "Protein! Protein! Tomorrow we eat protein!"

As I go out the door, my father snorts: "Sure, Drew, tomorrow I'll get a case a yogurt!"

At this moment, he and Nathan notice the watch on Raymond's wrist.

"Where'd you get that?" Nathan asks suspiciously.

Raymond of course plays dumb.

"What . . . ?"

CHAPTER SIX

I'VE BEEN SINGING NIGHTS AT THE ORCHID CLUB for nine months. It's for the experience, I keep reminding myself. Ya see, the Orchid Club is a topless joint. And Fat Floyd, the owner, hired me and my band, more or less for a gimmick, because none of the other joints in the area have live music. He pays us next to nothing, but I love to sing, although no one ever watches me. Everybody's always eyeballing the go-go girls. One of the girls is Delilah, and I'll tell ya something, she can dance. Plus, she's really a sweet girl. She lives in Jersey City and has an eight-year-old kid. Ya know, I know a lotta guys think, well, if a girl dances topless, she don't have much morals. But that really doesn't hold for Delilah. She's one of the sweetest people I know. I mean, she's not my type, but I like her and feel kinda protective toward her. Her husband deserted her when her kid was only three, and she's gotta make a livin' . . .

Sometimes we clown around while I sing. She fantasizes a lot too. She told me that while she's dancing she makes believe she's not there.

The crowd is pretty raunchy. A lotta drunks and droolers. I know it must be really degrading for her, but she don't take that G-string off, no sir, and she wears those little pasties on her, y'know, nipples. So it's like a really tiny bikini. That's one way of looking at it.

Geographically, the Orchid Club is laid out like most of these joints I've been in. At the end of the bar is a tiny area where the band plays. The go-go girls dance on the raised bar in front of the customers. My portable electric piano is set up front. I bought it for $65. It doesn't sound great, but in here who can tell. It's so noisy, I can barely hear myself sing. Even if this place was empty I could barely hear myself sing. You see, the club's located right off Route 3, a very busy highway. Big trucks and semis whip by all night long, grinding gears and mashing horns. Right around here is where the highway curves dangerously. I've been here ten months, and I figure the average is one and a half accidents per week. It's been nine days since there's been one. I figure we're about due.

Tonight, as usual, Petey, my drummer, is ripped, so he's drumming too fast. I'm gettin' annoyed. He does this all the time.

"Hey, Petey. Slow it down, huh?"

Petey looks up with stoned eyes. "What?"

Then Mark, my guitarist, pops a string and swears. "Just keep playin'," I tell him.

Mark looks up at me. "Whaddaya mean, keep playin'? I got no E-string."

Then Gino, the bass player who doubles on piano when I'm standing up singing, leans over as he pops a Sen-Sen in his mouth. He's always worried about his breath.

"Hey, Drew, what's the difference? You think they care?"

We all look out at the audience—Petey, Mark, Gino, and Fred, the sax player, and Gino's right, no one's lookin' at us. No one at all.

I try and raise everybody's spirits by breaking into a heavy rock number called "Drunk to a Punk." I wrote it one Friday afternoon while I was skipping stones down by the Hudson. I like to go down by the river, throw stones into the water and watch the rings swell. It's soothing . . . I usta go there after school a lot. Especially after gym class, I needed it. The river to me is like someone who listens . . .

See, it wasn't that I was a bad kid, or stupid. That wasn't why I was in the fourth division all my school years. It was just a matter of never caring about grades. Since I'm eight years old, I've wanted to become a singer. Math, science, and geography, none of those subjects were ever gonna help me land a job, so I never applied myself. I've always known I wanted to be a singer . . . Finally three years ago, I started doing something about it.

I'm singing my heart out when I notice

String enter. He smiles and waves at me. He's a friend of my father's. Well, not really a friend, actually, String is a professional weasel. He hangs in different places where connected people have a tendency to be and eavesdrops, trying to pick up a tip on a fixed horse race or a card game, or a dice shoot, or stolen goods to be fenced. Then he hurries over and tells my father about them. I personally don't care for him, but it's hard to hate the little guy. He's only about five-three, weighs about a hundred pounds, has false teeth, greasy hair, and is only about thirty-five, although he looks fifty. He does have a bad mouth though, and I don't dig guys that curse around women. Old-fashioned . . . all right, maybe I am a little, because I was brought up that way. I mean, you never swore around my mother. I remember once, this is funny, Raymond spit out a meat knish that my mother baked without knowing that the dough was bad, and he exclaimed, "Ahhh, this tastes like - - - -." My mother grabbed a bar of Ivory soap, pulled him over to the sink—Raymond was only nine then—and I mean she washed his mouth out!! Really scrubbed it, teeth an' all. She was great, my mother.

Cancer . . . I'd give anything, even my singing career, to be the man that discovers the cure for cancer.

Suddenly I notice Delilah's arguing with Fat Floyd over by the end of the bar. He's telling her something and she's shaking her head. He puts his hand on her arm and she removes it, then storms away. As she passes the stage, I reach down and stop her.

"What's wrong, Delilah?"

"Floyd wants me to dance naked."

"What?"

"He wants me to take off everything. Y'know I'm no stripper, Drew!"

"Wait a minute." I turn to the band, tell them I'll be right back, climb off the stage, and escort Delilah back to Fat Floyd, who's sucking on a moist El Producto.

"Whaddaya doin'? Get back on the stage," Fat Floyd says.

"What's goin' on?" I say.

He points to Delilah. "She don't wanna take off her G-string! It's not hidin' nothin', Drew, I don't know why she don't wanna take it off."

"Because ya didn't hire her to dance nude, that's why she don't wanna take it off."

"I only dance topless. You know that," Delilah spits out angrily.

Fat Floyd shrugs. "Listen, Delilah, sweetheart, all my competition's topless. I gotta stay one step ahead of the future. It's progress. I mean, look at the magazines, ya got *Penthouse, Gallery, Hustler*—nude is the wave of the future, honey."

A few of the guys in the crowd hear Floyd and roar their approval. Fat Floyd opens his arms to the crowd. "See, they want it. A good businessman's gotta cater to his clientele."

"Well, I don't!" Delilah snaps.

The crowd boos!

Fat Floyd turns away from Delilah. "Then you're fired; bye."

She walks away in a huff. Floyd then turns to a new dancer who has just stepped on the bar to take her turn.

"Take it off, sweetheart." He turns back to me. "Go on, get back up there, Drew."

"No way."

"What?"

"I'm not workin' in a meat joint. I quit." I turn around and walk away.

"Where are ya goin'? Ya better get back up there!"

I look up at the band. They know where I'm at. As we pack up, the crowd boos.

Then all of a sudden, *screech, skid, honk, crash!* Less than a hundred yards from the club, a drunk driver coming back from New York skids into a doughnut truck . . .

I unlock the door and walk in the house. I don't know why I call the apartment a house. I just always have.

As usual the television is on. The station is signing off with the national anthem and my grandfather's asleep on the couch. I turn off the TV, find a blanket and cover him. I turn out the light and walk into the kitchen. My old man's asleep at the kitchen table. There's a half-empty gallon of dark wine by his side and he was in the middle of handicapping tomorrow's winners with the racing form that he Scotchtaped together.

I poke him, he doesn't move. . . . I jab him again.

"C'mon, c'mon, wake up . . ."

He lifts his head off the table and grunts at me through bleary eyes, then stumbles down the hallway and turns into his bedroom. I follow him, walk past his room and enter my room which I share with Raymond. Raymond fell asleep reading a magazine. I pick it up and check it—*Swank*. I examine the centerfold. The girl's not bad. I flip through it quickly and then throw it in the trash.

"Hey, it had an article in it I was readin' for school." Raymond's awake.

"Yeah, about what?"

"What it says I'm goin' through. How come I get these cramps is that I need a release. The article was full of important information about puberty . . ."

I look at Raymond. He nods. I fish out the magazine.

"Yeah, what page was this article?"

"It's the centerfold."

I toss it back in the trash.

"C'mon, she'll get wrinkled."

"Go to sleep or I'll wrinkle you!"

He grumbles and rolls over. . . . I slip off my jacket, and the Record Your Own Voice record falls out. I pick it up and I walk over to the shelf and place my two hundred and fifty-third record on the stack. Then I take out my wallet and start emptying my pockets on the dresser, which is what I do every night, so I don't misplace things. I find the Western coin in my hand, with "Rosemarie Lemon" stamped on it. For some reason, something Raymond said echoes in my ears.

"The article was fulla important information about puberty," Raymond said.

Information! I jump to my feet. It never occurred to me! Maybe she just moved here!

I hurry down the hall into the kitchen, grab the phone and I dial 411. Finally she comes on. "Excuse me, information?"

"Information, yes?"

"You gotta new number for a Lemon, a Rosemarie Lemon, somewhere in the city? One 'm', like in lemonade."

I hear her flip through the pages.

"Yes, I do."

"Great!"

"The number is 555–1415."

"Could ya give me the address?"

"I'm sorry, we're not allowed to give out addresses."

"How about this one time?"

"I'm sorry, we're not allowed to give out addresses."

"Could you bend a little? It's very important. Urgent, as a matter of fact. I want to see her in person rather than call her."

I hear a touch of humanity in her voice as she asks, "You wanna surprise her, huh?"

"If you give me her address, I can. Who knows, you might be responsible for an important change in my life."

"You sound desperate." she laughs.

"I am," I laugh back, and now I know she'll give it to me. I grab a match cover and pencil.

"Okay, here's the address."

I copy it down. It's not far away, in the nicer section of town.

"Thanks a lot, I really appreciate it."

I hang up, pad back into my bedroom and lay down with a smile on my face. Rosemarie Lemon . . . what's she like, I wonder, as I decide to rest up a little before I get up, get undressed, wash my face and brush my teeth. I'll just lay here a minute . . .

The next morning of course I wake up fully dressed.

CHAPTER SEVEN

BEFORE I ENTER HER BUILDING, I RUN MY FINGERS through my hair. It's a nice building. Only a coupla years old. Much nicer than the one I live in.

Not unhappily I notice there's an Out of Order sign hanging on the front of the elevator. I find her name in the directory, and climb three flights of steps, but not before checking to see if the stairwell door will lock behind me. As I travel down the hallway, I'm rotating the "Rosemarie Lemon" coin over my knuckles. I learned to do it without even realizing it.

I step up to the door and knock. It sounds silly, but my heart is beating fast.

A young woman's voice calls from inside.

"Who's there?"

"Rosemarie?"

"Who's there?"

I buff the toe of my right boot on my left pants leg as I answer, "Ah . . . remember the guy from, ah, the train station, yesterday?"

I hear footsteps approach the door. She's right on the other side of the door, I can tell. I hear her breathing, and for a second I wonder what her breath will taste like on our first kiss.

"Who?" she says.

I smile. "It's me, y'know, the singer."

"Who's that?" a gruff male voice asks the girl as he approaches the door.

"I don't know, Rufus."

The door opens, and suddenly I'm facing a huge black man with shoulders so wide I think he probably has to enter his apartment sideways. He's standing behind the young black girl, who's probably his wife.

"Rufus? You're Rufus Lemon?"

He looks down at me and scowls.

"Yeah, who are you?"

I smile . . .

"I'm—I'm on my way," I say and I was.

I drive to the store, park in front, and amble inside. Nathan is behind the sewing machine, stitching a button on somebody's coat. He looks up at me and grabs a piece of paper.

"We get three pounds of ground beef," he says, reading from his list. "Lean, a sack of potatoes, we get cauliflower, lettuce, tomatoes, and cucumbers for a salad. We get whole wheat bread, that's healthy, lotsa protein."

My father, who's operating the steam press in the background, sees me and comes forward.

"Hey, where ya been, we gotta very important pick-up."

Nathan turns around. "I'm talking, you interrupted me."

"Did you meet her?" my father asks me.

"Meet who?" Nathan asks. "Who'd he meet?"

"I didn't meet anybody," I say.

Nathan looks at my father. "Whaddaya saying? He met somebody?"

"He's always on the lookout for Miss Dream Girl, isn't he?"

"Ah, why don'tcha go in the corner and chase yourself?" Nathan says.

"Did your nose come with those glasses? I'm talkin' to my son here," my father says, then turns his head toward me. I notice a ladder of creases on his neck.

"Your drummer Petey called. He says you guys got fired last night?"

"I didn't get fired, I quit."

"You're not working at the Orchid Club anymore?" Nathan asks, concerned.

"Nah, Floyd turned the place into a strip joint, so I quit. I'm a singer, not a burlesque comic."

Nathan feels bad. "Ah, that's really a pity."

"It's all right." I shrug. "I was only treading water there anyway."

"Okay, so look," my father says, "what the important pick-up is all about is Mr. Patterson seems to be unhappy with the service he's been gettin' from Victory Cleaners, so they wanna try us."

"Us? Why us?"

"I don't know." He shakes his head. "I guess he heard we were good."

"Who told him that lie?" I say.

"That's what *I* said," Nathan says, biting the thread off a button.

My father shrugs. "Look, who cares? This could be a big account. Y'know Mr. Patterson also owns the Capri Lounge and all the Moonshot Pizzerias . . ." He looks towards the door. "Hi, Helen, you're late!"

Helen, an attractive brunette in her late forties, enters. She's a long-time employee, and has been my father's girlfriend for the last five months.

"I overslept. Hiya Nate, hiya Drew."

"How are ya, Helen? Nice dress," Nathan remarks.

"Thank you."

"What were ya doin' last night?" my father asks her.

"I was busy . . . Coffee on?" she says as she walks toward the back.

"Yeah, I put it on an hour ago," Nathan tells her.

"Busy doin' what?" my father says.

Helen doesn't answer, and I can see the old man start to go through a change. He definitely likes Helen. Love no, but he cares about her. Helen's from Montclair. It's about a half hour from here, located in the middle of the state. When she first started working here she used to commute in her brand new Buick Skylark. She doesn't really need the work. She's divorced, and from what I understand she got a pretty good settlement. She's bored though. She and my old man met at the race track. They were both with different people. He was with a local girl and she was with her brother. They struck up a friendly conversation in front of the five-dollar show window. My father picked her two winners, and from that day on they started seeing each other. As it turned out, her ex-husband was right in the middle of selling their house, so when she relocated she took a place not far away in Jersey City. My old man spends at least one, two nights a week there. It's a very strange relationship. They're very wrong for each other as I see it, 'cause they're so much alike. They're both very hot-blooded and hot-tempered, but then again they're both lonely, and I guess it's companionship.

My father turns back to me, wanting to finish up fast so he can go back and talk to Helen.

"Look, Patterson's trade could keep this place from goin' under. You know, Pinky works there and I know you wanna talk to him 'bout Johnny playin' poker with Raymond. Just don't get into an argument. Hold your temper. We could use the business."

Suddenly the back of my neck feels hot.

"Did ya hear what I said?" he asks again.

"Yeah, I heard."

CHAPTER EIGHT

As I DRIVE UP ROUTE 3 TOWARD PATTERSON'S Landmark, I start thinking about Pinky. Pinky's a Leo, too. He's three days older than me and that's why I don't believe in astrology. We have no similar characteristics. At least I hope not. Other than the fact that we were born one block away from each other, went to the same school, traveled in the fourth division together, were close friends for a while, and both have younger brothers, we have absolutely nothing in common. Johnny De Soto, his younger brother, is the one who Raymond is playing poker with. Nothing terribly wrong with that, except number one, Johnny's eighteen years old and Raymond's only fifteen, and number two, I can't prove it but I'm sure Johnny cheats. Which relates to what went sour between me and Pinky. He's always out for the fast buck and he doesn't care who he steps on to get it. When he was sixteen, he started veering off in this direction and about that time we drifted apart.

"Laundry?" I say to the cook, as I enter through the back way and walk through the kitchen.

"Inside," he waves his head, as he pours a huge pot of clams into a kettle of boiling water.

I walk through two swinging doors, into a restaurant area, as it is being set up for lunch. I'm not there two seconds, before I hear that sarcastic voice.

"Hey, hey. The singer . . ."

I turn around and Pinky (Louis) De Soto sways across the room, wearing a new suit, a crooked smile and loud taps on the heels of his new black leather Florsheims. His bad complexion is looking a little worse these days—I guess he's been pickin' at his face—and he's got on those two gaudy pinky rings as usual. These days when I look at him, I'm amazed we were ever so close as kids.

"Long time no see," he says as he polishes the emerald pinky ring on the lapel of his suit jacket.

"How are ya, Pinky?" I ask unenthusiastically.

"Ah, life is great at the top," he snickers. "This suit cost three hundred dollars." He starts to model it. "The shirt, thirty-five; tie, twenty. Shoes cost me seventy-five . . ."

"You oughta get yourself insured." I laugh. Pinky doesn't.

"I like your T-shirt, Drew," he says, and reaches over toward it.

I push his hand away. "So do I."

I get down to business.

"Listen, Pinky, your little brother's been strong armin' Raymond."

"Johnny's not so little."

"What's he doin' playin' poker with an eighth grader? He can't find guys his own speed?"

"Raymond's a wiseguy, he asked to play."

"Well, you tell your brother, the debt's called off and leave Raymond alone."

"You tellin' me what to do?" He tightens.

"I'm tellin' you the debt's called off."

"Don't tell me what to do."

"Okay, I'm informin' you. Does that sound better, Pinky? I'm informin' you."

"You're informin' me?" he says, trying to look shocked.

"Yeah, I'm informin' you to inform your brother." I walk away. "Now where's the laundry?"

Pinky lights a cigarette with a gold monogrammed lighter. "Y'know, Drew, it's funny the way things turned out. Remember the good old days? We grew up together, we graduated together—"

I cut him off. "Nah, Pinky, I don't wanna hear your crap."

He flares up. "Crap! Well, let's look at where we are now! I'm here in a three hundred dollar suit with five hundred dollars in my pocket and where are you? Huh? You're where? You're nowhere!"

I turn around and look at him. I'm hot but I restrain myself.

"What is it with you, Pinky? Why do you got all these problems?"

He knows he's made me angry and he enjoys it.

"Hey, Drew, y'know who recommended your cleaners to Mr. Patterson? It was me. And y'know why? C'mon, ask me why."

I don't answer him.

"'Cause my laundry goes out with the help's and I just love the idea of you washin' my stained underwear."

He breaks out laughing, as a voice calls: "Louis!"

"Yeah?" Pinky turns. It's Ned, Mr. Patterson's bodyguard. A very large Italian, with a Fu Manchu moustache.

"Mr. Patterson wants to see ya."

"Right now?"

"Let's go, Pinky."

"Wait here," he orders me and follows Ned into a big, empty room.

Of course I don't wait. I trail along just because he told me not to.

We enter a room which is under construction. I don't know what they're building, but it looks like they're building a stage up in front.

Mr. Patterson, the man who owns this club, steps out from behind the new bar. He's a tall black man with a thin moustache. His clothes are custom tailored and he possesses a commanding presence. It's very strange that Pinky works for Mr. Patterson because as long as I've known him, he's hated blacks.

"Who's he?" Patterson asks.

Pinky turns around and sees me. "Whaddaya doin' here? I told ya to wait in the other room."

He turns back to his boss.

"He's the delivery boy." He turns back to me. "Alright, go get the laundry. It's downstairs."

"Don't you sing at the Orchid Club?" Mr. Patterson asks, seeming to recognize me.

I'm surprised. "You been there?"

Pinky snaps, "Mr. Patterson owns that building."

"No, I'm not working there anymore," I say. "Fat Floyd turned the place into a strip joint."

Pinky snaps again. "Don't you think Mr. Patterson knows that! He owns that building!"

Patterson tells Pinky to relax, then sweeps his eyes across the room.

"Do you know what I'm doing to this room, Drew?"

"Expanding?"

Patterson nods. He finds a loose thread on his sleeve. "I'm gonna turn this room into a disco, but with live music."

"Really?"

"Yep," he says. "Seafood and music. Can you think of a better combination?"

"No, I think it's a great idea, really."

"Glad you like it." He smiles, then turns to Pinky. "Give him the laundry and come right up, Louis. I have some errands for you."

"Right away." Pinky nods.

Mr. Patterson heads toward the stairs to the second floor.

"Mr. Patterson," I stutter. He turns. "Do you have a group booked to play here yet?"

"Not yet. Can you recommend one?"

Patterson's teasing me. Pinky grins.

"Look, Mr. Patterson, you couldn't tell from the Orchid Club, but we gotta hot sound, Mr. Patterson. My group, The New Jersey Turnpike, we're hot!"

"Hot?"

"Can we audition?"

He mulls it over for a second, then shrugs.

"Sure, call tomorrow. Ask for Mr. Redmond. If he doesn't have too many other acts on the list, why not?"

He climbs the stairs to the second floor.

Pinky turns back to me. This time I smile. Pinky's sizzling.

"Mr. Patterson was just bein' polite."

"Better show me the laundry. I don't wanna hold up your *errands*."

"I don't know what you're smilin' about, your singin' is nothin' to be happy about!"

Then it dawns on me!

"Why Louis, you're jealous!" I say, smiling.

"Jealous of you?! You better go down an' pick up my underwear."

I get serious and give him a last warning.
"Just tell your brother the debt's called off."

"No, you tell—"

I cut him off.

"No. You tell him!" I walk away before
he has a chance to say anything.

I open the doors of the van to chuck the
bundle of laundry in, and outta the corner of
my eye, I see *her*. My heart stops.

It's *Rosemarie*.

She's watching the bus as it pulls up.

"Rosemarie!"

I run outta the parkin' lot into the street
Boom!

I rebound right off a stationwagon's fen-
der! I get up, but the driver, a hard-hat, leaps
out of a construction firm's Ford and grabs me
by the arm.

"It's okay, it's okay, I'm not hurt," I say.

"You ran right in fronta me!"

"Yeah, it's alright, forget it!"

I wanna get to Rosemarie. She's boarding
the bus.

He still holds on.

"You one of those bums goin' aroun' fallin'
down in front of cars for insurance?"

"What?"

"You heard me."

"Let go of my arm!"

"I ain't payin' a nickel, I got witnesses!"

He stops a woman going by with a shop-
ping bag.

"You, you seen it! Right, ma'am? Not a cent I'm payin'. I know this bum's racket."

The bus pulls away.

"I oughta make a citizen's arrest," he threatens, squeezing my arm tight.

"You've got one more second to let go."

"Then what?" he sneers.

The temper goes. Before I know it, I hit him in the mouth. He bangs into a telephone pole. Then leaps back on me. All two hundred and twenty some pounds of him. I grab him in a headlock as he tries to brush my teeth on the curb. As a police car screeches up, a crowd forms.

Out jumps Ronnie's twin brother Ricky and another cop named Pete. They yank us apart and Ricky turns to me, half smiling. He loves fights. He says hello, asks me how the career's going, then addresses both of us.

"I'll make it real simple," he says. "We can stand here and figure out who caused what and why, or we can go down to the station and one or both of you can press charges—or you can both shake hands, don't tell me anything and go on your merry ways."

Being an alumnus of at least a hundred fights, Ricky knows ninety-nine percent of scuffles between strangers are for ridiculous reasons, so he doesn't want to even hear about this one.

The hard-hat's on his lunch break. No one wants to hang around.

We shake hands.

CHAPTER NINE

THAT NIGHT, SINCE I DON'T HAVE TO BE AT WORK, I go to see Korina, the gypsy. Some people go to see a psychiatrist when they're confused or upset—me, I go see Korina. She's a dark, very intense woman in her late thirties. She's got long black hair and big black eyes. We've known each other a long time. I consider her a close friend, though we've never been romantically involved. I never made the overture because I know she's not really my type. She's not the right one and I wouldn't want to have sex with her just because it means a lot to me to have somebody I can talk to.

Korina's very quiet as she flips over the Tarot cards.

"I see another fight in your future."

"Great," I say sarcastically.

She looks up at me. "A bigger one."

I watch carefully as she flips over the Princess.

"Over a woman."

"Over a woman?"

Korina sets the deck of cards down and takes my palm. She studies it for what seems a long time. Then she looks up to me.

"You didn't tell me about her, Drew. This woman was the cause of your fight today."

"In a way, kind of . . . "

I'm dying to know what she's getting at but she always works slowly, so I've learned to be patient.

"She's different," Korina says, studying the cards.

And then before I know it, I'm telling her about Rosemarie.

"Light brown hair down to here, big blue eyes, very sensitive-looking, I tell ya Korina, when I saw her somethin' happened. I can't get her off my mind. I see other girls an' I thinka her."

She looks up at me with those deep round eyes. Sometimes I feel she can see into my brain.

"I've never heard you talk like this!"

I take the coin out of my wallet and I set it on the table. She studies it.

"Rosemarie Lemon . . . Rosemarie Lemon has two meanings."

I lean forward in the folding chair. It wobbles so I jam the edge of my sneaker under it.

"Rose—pure as a rose. Marie—remember. Her name means—remember purity."

I can't help smiling.

"What has this girl done to you?" Korina asks.

"I've never even talked to her."

She pushes the Tarot cards to me. "Shuffle."

I shuffle them.

"Spread them."

I spread them out.

"Pick seven."

I select the cards very, very carefully. Then she gives me a patient look. For a second she looks like the Mona Lisa.

"Count them."

Not understanding why, I count them. Eight cards. I reshuffle the deck and spread the cards again.

"Seven," she says.

"I know, I know."

I select the cards and hand them to her. She arranges the cards in a T pattern. The Princess falls at the head of the T. She stares at it.

"It's an omen. It's not meant you should meet her yet."

"Why not?"

"You're not ready for her."

"Why, whaddaya mean?"

She taps the Princess and looks at me. A touch of hurt in her eyes. A touch of envy.

"This girl is very special," she says quietly.

"I know," I nod.

"No." She shakes her head. "She's more special than even you think. Rosemarie Lemon is a world of her own."

She takes my palm between her hands. "Things happen when they are meant to happen. Don't torture yourself, Drew."

"I don't understand."

After a pause, she says, "You will." Then she collects the cards and says, without looking at me: "Goodnight."

I stand up, confused, and thank her. She nods, still not looking up, and I leave through the beaded curtain. As I leave, she turns over the deck. . . . The Princess is on the bottom.

As I walk Raymond to school the next morning, I can't get Rosemarie Lemon off my mind. I know there's something very special about her. I can't stop thinkin'. . . . Maybe she's the right one.

As Raymond and I take stools at the White Castle, I discuss yesterday's fight with him, trying to infuse the incident with a significance I think he might benefit from.

"Ya see," I say, "ya see, Ray, you gotta look at bad experiences from the What did I learn from this side. Because the main object of life is not to make the same mistake someone else made." I turn to the counterman.

"Give me four hard-boiled eggs, okay, Julio?"

"I want a cherry Danish!" Ray exclaims reaching for one.

"Ya need protein," I tell him, pulling his

hand away. I pay the counterman for four eggs and hand Raymond two.

"Put one in your pocket for later."

He follows my instructions and we pad down the sidewalk, peeling eggs.

"So, if somebody was sprayin' his bad breath in your face over nothin', would you explode an' punch him out, or would you turn around and walk away?"

Raymond thinks it over for a second . . . He looks up at me with a grin.

"I'd look both ways before I crossed the street."

I give him a look. He finishes the rest of his egg and wipes some yolk from his mouth. The kid is such a wiseguy. But y'know—he's right. We walk on and school looms into view.

Suddenly he stops, nervous.

"Drew—I don't got today's installment."

I look at him.

"I owe Johnny a lotta money. If I miss an installment, Johnny said he and the Warriors'll blacken my eyes.

"How much you owe 'im?"

"I signed an I.O.U. for a hundred dollars."

I look at my brother. I can't believe it!

"Johnny kept raisin'," Raymond explains. "I didn't think he was serious. We laughed about it. Next day I come to school and he says, 'Where's the money?' "

"How much you paid?" I demand to know.

"He has a whole gang behind him." Ray's talking a mile a minute. "You don't know what

83

it's like, walking around those halls. Every time I pass one of 'em they punch me in the arm to make sure my memory don't go stale." He whips off his jacket and pulls up his shirt sleeve. He's got a discolored map of black an' blue on his right arm, right below the shoulder. I know how hard Johnny had to hit Raymond to make a black and blue mark that big. I feel the heat on the back of my neck. I increase my pace.

"Whaddaya gonna do?" Raymond says.

"I'm gonna settle it! Let's go."

Suddenly I stop! There *she* is, standing across the street at the bus stop. Raymond tries to figure out what I'm looking at. He sees Rosemarie. She looks so beautiful. And she's carrying books.

"Wow! Who is she?" Raymond asks.

I just stand there. I can't answer. Then the words seem to come from nowhere . . .

"Raymond—tell Johnny you're not payin' another cent. I'll meet ya after school: I'll take care of it then."

Before I know it, I'm drifting across the street. I hear Raymond from afar . . .

"Wow—beautiful."

I'm crossing the street and Rosemarie is watching me . . . But there's something, something in her eyes. It looks like she wants to meet me, but at the same time doesn't want to meet me. It's hard to explain but I can feel strong indecisiveness going on inside her.

"Hi," I say as I step up on the curb.

She smiles nervously and nods. As she

walks with the line to board the bus, I walk along.

"I'm Drew—you're Rosemarie, right?"

She just nods again.

I'm very confused.

"Listen, all I want to do is meet you . . . What's the matter?"

She looks away. I touch her arm and smile.

"Hey, I'm a nice guy. Look, remember this?" I pull the coin out of my pocket. The Rosemarie Lemon coin.

"You want it back? Tell ya what. Just help me break the ice an' I'll give it back."

She looks back at me like she doesn't hear a word I'm saying. Now, I've been ignored before but usually I know why. I'm starting to think this girl is just very stuck up. I feel like saying something nasty as she steps up into the bus, but then a very strange thing happens.

The bus driver sees Rosemarie, smiles, and then says, "Good morning." In sign language! ! !

It all hits me. All at once it hits me! Oh my God! Rosemarie *is* special.

She's deaf.

I stand there, stunned. I watch her move down the aisle and take a window seat as the bus pulls away.

Suddenly I take off after it. I run alongside it. She watches me. I smile and wave at her. I've never run so fast.

Bam! I run right into a parking meter! I

double over in pain. It hurts so bad. I got myself right in the solar plexus. I breathe deep and force myself to keep going, 'cause the bus just pulled over. I board it up ahead at the next stop. I step up to the exact change meter, panting. I dig into my pocket . . . I don't have the right change.

"All I got's a five," I say to the bus driver as he rotates the steering wheel to the left and the bus belches out gas and pulls away from the curb.

"You'll have to get off at the next stop then."

I turn around and look at the passengers. "Excuse me, does anybody have change of a five?"

A woman checks her purse and a man digs in his pocket, but neither has change. I just jam the five dollar bill into the machine and walk down the aisle. I sit in the empty seat next to Rosemarie. She looks at me, then stares straight ahead. I take out the Rosemarie Lemon coin and put it in her hands. It's an awkward moment. I don't know what to say. I never met a deaf girl before. In fact, the only experience I've had with a deaf person was when a grungy guy on the subway handed me a card with the deaf alphabet on it and held out his palm for a handout. I gave him a quarter and that was it. That's the only contact I've had with these people.

I can feel the bus driver keeping a protective eye on Rosemarie through the rear-view mirror.

I tap her on the hand. She looks at me.

"You don't hear me at all?"

She shakes her head.

Then she points down to my stomach, looking at me questioningly.

"Oh, I'm fine."

She nods, then smiles. I don't know what to say again. Suddenly the bus seems much noisier: I become very aware of every sound. The lady on the other side, the one that dug into her purse to see if she had change for me, she has a crying baby in her lap. And there's a kid, a few feet away, playing with one of those crank toys. I look around. Two senior citizens are arguing in the back. I realize, my God, she doesn't hear any of this. What's it like, I think for a moment. Not to hear at all? To live in a totally silent world?

I notice her pulling the bus cord. She gets up, I stand up and let her by.

She walks down the aisle, waves to the driver, then steps out the back door . . . I follow her out.

We're standing in front of the Hoboken Parochial School for the Deaf. "You go here?" I ask.

She nods. I look at a group of children waiting by the steps to the school.

"Oh, you teach those kids?"

She nods again.

"She one of yours?" I point to this really beautiful little black girl, a hearing aid in her ear, standing alone on the steps, apart from the others. She's waving at Rosemarie. Rosemarie waves back and does some sign language to her. I wish I knew what the hell she's saying. I feel so left out. She turns to me and then mimes singing into a pencil. She seems a little more relaxed now that she's on her own turf. I understand what she's asking and I'm glad she's initiated some conversation.

"Oh, yeah, I'm a singer. What I was doin' in the recordin' booth, was, see I usta have a tape recorder..."

She stops me. She gestures and mouths the word, "Slowly."

"Ohh, I'm talkin' too fast for you to read my lips? Is that right?"

She nods.

I talk slowly. "Must be hard to read lips. Ya must miss alot, huh?"

She shrugs. We just stare at each other for a moment. Some of the little girls come over and watch us, curiously. Rosemarie checks her watch, then mouths the word, "Goodbye," and heads for the school, surrounded by her kids.

I follow and on the steps I stop her.

"Can I call you?"

As soon as the words come out of my mouth, I want to fling myself under a steamroller. She looks at me and humors me with a smile.

"Oh yeah, right," I say.

She nods, then walks up the stairs and enters the school...

For a moment I just stand there, not knowing what to do. But I just can't leave. Alright, she's deaf. What does that mean? She can't hear, but so what, she's still who she is. And I still want to know who she is. All of a sudden, I'm snapped out of my thoughts by a barking dog that chases a squirrel up a tree. I run into the building after her. But the hall is empty.

I wander around, then come to a door that says

ADULT SOCIAL CLUB

I walk in and it's so *loud*. Twenty or so deaf people are standing around, involved in different activities. A couple of them are watching "A.M. America" on the television, which is blaring. A radio is on full volume. A few people are playing checkers, talking to each other in weird monotone voices.

Somebody taps me on the shoulder. I turn, jolted.

"Ow you lubbing for? Can I helb you?" a man with thin hair asks.

"No, no," I say as I back out of the door.

I walk outside, quick.

A thousand thoughts are flooding through my mind as I amble toward the street.

Rosemarie is watching me from her classroom on the second floor. Then she turns around to face her class of rowdy deaf and hard-of-hearing fourth graders. The kids are signing and talking with each other in those strange high-pitched voices, and I guess if you didn't know they were deaf, you'd think they were retarded. She flicks the lights on and off, captures their attention, and orders them to take their seats. The beautiful little black girl is still standing by the window. Rosemarie claps her hands hard. The girl turns and points across the street. Rosemarie walks back to the window and sees that she's looking at me. The little girl circles her face with her palm and grins. Rosemarie nods with a sad look on her face.

Later, I find out that's the sign that means handsome . . .

CHAPTER TEN

I'M IN THE DRY CLEANER REMOVING THE PATTER-son's Landmark uniforms from the dry washer. My father's on the steam iron and Helen's plastic-bagging shirts. Nathan's up front at the counter tending to a Cuban customer. I overhear my father talking to Helen.

"So Helen, ya still didn't tell me where you were last night. I called twice."

Without turning, Helen says, "I went out."

"With who?" my father asks, growing tense.

"A person."

My old man gives me a look, then looks back at Helen. "Whattaya botherin' with fly-weights for?"

"How do you know what he's like?" she snaps.

"He's a skinny weasel that chews spiders and shoulda been smothered in his crib."

My father brings the steam iron down on a shirt. Helen smiles to herself. He coos. "Wanna see a movie tonight?"

"He already asked me out," Helen says with her back still to my father.

He blows up. "Alright, well then, forget it, huh, forget I asked! All of a sudden you're datin' a million guys . . . " He holds the steam press down too long and burns a customer's blouse. He looks at the hole and sizzles . . .

Helen comes over. Her voice is soft. "You really care about me, don't you, Frank?"

He's angry. "I don't care about you."

She touches his neck and flirts. "What movie?"

My old man turns and gives her a half angry, half happy look. I watch, feel lonely, and think about this morning and Rosemarie Lemon.

"Y'know, Helen," my father says as he brushes a wave of Helen's brown hair off her forehead, "you'd look great as a blonde."

"A blonde? You really think so?" She checks herself in the small dusty mirror on the wall.

"Sure." Frank nods, coming up behind her and circling her waist with his arms. "Blondes have more fun."

Suddenly the front door is yanked open, and I hear the familiar voice of the weasel.

"Where's Frank? I gotta talk to him!"

"He's not in," Nathan tells him.

"Frank, Frank, you there?" the squeaky voice excitedly calls out, ignoring Nathan.

Frank releases Helen and ambles up front. He shoots Nathan an aggravated look, then turns and faces String, who's trying to catch his breath.

"Sorry to burst in like that, but I got news, you won't believe the news I got," String says.

"That I'm sure of," Nathan says. He shows the Cuban the shirt he's finished tailoring for him. He points to the darts in the back of the shirt.

"I had to take it in from the back. If I took it in from the sides, it would pull under the armpits, ya understand?"

"Si!" The Cuban nods and pays my grandfather five dollars and leaves.

String, who is waiting for the Cuban to leave, blurts out to Helen:

"Hi Helen, ya lookin' pretty as always. Hey, Drew, what happened, you're not workin' at Fat Floyd's anymore?"

"Get outta here, why don't ya, String, huh?"

"Hey, y'know I'm a fan a yours!"

"Ya got another hot racing tip, String?" I ask. "Like the one that lost my father two hundred dollars last month?"

Upset String turns and looks at my father. "Hey, you didn't tell 'im, Frank?"

"Tell 'im what?" Nathan asks.

"I gave your father a tip that won 'im six an' a half yards last week. An' for nothin', I gave 'im that tip to make up for before."

93

Nathan shakes his head at my father.

"I shoulda known you didn't pick those horses yourself!"

String waves away at the air with his hands. "Forget that. Listen to this! Last night, I'm in the men's room at Floyd's—stinking hole!—but what a tip I overheard as I was squattin' on the john with my legs up so no one'd know I was there."

"Hey, String!" I sneer. The guy has no pride whatsoever.

"Anyway . . . " he continues, "last night I overheard two hoods from Jersey City whisperin' about a fixed race! ! !" He slaps himself in the face.

"A banana race today at Monmouth," he says, almost religiously, looking at my father with wide, bloodshot eyes.

My father freezes. "You sure?" His voice rises in the same hushed, reverent tone.

"On my mother, I swear I heard it with my own ears! I'm goin' aroun' tryin' to raise every nickel I can—I sold my motor scooter. The horse is such a friggin' long shot, the big boys don't wanna touch the odds! It's a very private affair!"

He places his hand on his heart and whispers very dramatically. "I'm tellin' ya Frank . . . this is it—this is get rich day! I've never had a tip like this!"

My father gets down to business. "How much for the name of the horse?"

"Well now, don't freak when you hear the price 'cause what I'm doin' for ya is gonna change your financial life." String's voice is suddenly cool.

"How much, ya squirrel?"

"Fifty," says String.

My father explodes. "Fifty dollars you charge a friend that's lent you money when you were down!"

He grabs String by the neck. Me and my grandfather have to yank him off. String backs away, gasping. The old man breaks loose, runs over and closes the front door, preventing String from leaving.

"Make it five dollars or you don't leave here alive," he says, red-faced.

"Frank," String pleads nervously, running a finger through his Brylcreamed hair, "I'm only tryin' to raise money. Yer gonna make a fortune!"

"What if you're wrong?" my father spits out, gritting his teeth.

"Rip my eyes out! Slit my throat!" String pulls out his top row of teeth and sets the bridge-work on the counter.

"Drop 'em in the Hudson if this horse don't win by ten lengths ! ! !"

Nathan and I are sitting in the van as my father comes out of the Hoboken Savings and Loan with a wad of cash in his hand. He steps into a phone booth and makes a quick call. Me and Nathan look at each other. Nathan shakes his head in disgust. We both know who he's calling. He's calling Mr. Giasullo. It's not enough he's going to the track, he's also gotta place a bet with the bookie.

"Who'd you call?" Nathan asks, knowing the answer. Frank climbs into the van and lights up one of the cigars which he reserves for when he goes to the track. He ignores the question, 'cause he knows Nathan is baiting him.

I'm behind the wheel, and we're heading toward the Garden State Parkway.

"The weather . . ." my old man says as he exhales a mouthful of smoke. "It's gonna be sunny an' warm. The track'll be fast."

"Yeah, sure," Nathan says, as he leans over and rolls down Frank's window. "How much ya take out?"

"Enough," my father says.

"How much is enough?" I ask. I swerve the van to the left, just missing a stray cat with almost no tail.

"Plenty."

"I hope you're not bein' stupid," Nathan says.

"For once I'm bein' very smart."

"Good—so how much?" my grandfather asks again.

"Don't you like surprises?" my father smiles.

"I had the last surprise I want years ago from your mother."

"Yeah, and what was that?" Frank asks.

Nathan looks at me and then back at my father.

"You."

I laugh.

Nathan and I have settled into our seats at the track. I look back over my shoulder and sweep my eyes over the packed grandstands. If Rosemarie were here right now, I think, all she would see is a mass of flapping mouths.

I stick my fingers in my ears, turning my head from side to side. It's weird. It really is weird.

There's a tug on my sleeve. Nathan's staring at me.

"What're you doin'?" he says. I am reading his lips. It's even stranger to look at him talk, see his lips move, and not hear what he's saying.

I unplug my ears.

"What're you doin'?" Nathan says, poking me.

"My ears are dirty."

He looks at me quizzically. "You feelin' alright?"

"Yeah, sure. Hey, how much you tell Dad to bet for you?"

"I'm not betting. You?" he asks, as he watches the horses parade by.

"I'm only here to look out for Raymond's college money," I say.

All of a sudden, Nathan's face pales. He checks the form, looks up, checks the form again. A very raggedy-looking beast is walking to the starting gate. The color is draining from his face.

"Am I nuts," he asks, "or does number five look like a farm horse?"

I look at number five. "Yeah. And what's the matter with it, you think? It's already sweating." It dawns on me. "That's not Sleepwalker?"

Nathan doesn't answer, which is my answer. I grab the form and check it. Compared to the other thoroughbreds, Sleepwalker looks like a used washrag.

At that moment, my father comes down the aisle, grinning.

"Look. Number five! That's Sleepwalker ! ! !" I grab his shoulders.

He lifts his worn binoculars to his eyes and calmly watches the wretched-looking beast enter the gate. For some insane reason, he smiles confidently.

"I know."

"You know? ? ! !"

"Look, relax. Here, smoke a cigar. Take in the sights." He relights his cigar, which is beginning to unravel in his mouth.

"How much you bet?" I ask, astonished.

Very dramatically, he lifts his hand out of his suit jacket and fans out what looks like at least thirty one hundred-dollar win tickets. No place or show, all wins! *All one hundred dollar wins ! ! !* My grandfather's eyes almost fall outta their sockets. My mouth suddenly goes dry.

"Twenty-seven hundred," my father says.

"When you were two years old," Nathan says, shaking his head in disgust, "you plugged your nostrils with bubble gum and we had to rush you to the hospital. I asked the doctor, 'Why would he do something like that? Could it be a sign of retardation?' The doctor said you were just a curious baby, but I was never convinced. . . . Now—I'm convinced." He shouts, *"You are retarded ! !"*

The track announcer's voice comes over

the loudspeaker. "The horses are in the gate. The flag is up, waiting on Sleepwalker . . ."

I look over. Sleepwalker is bucking. "What's wrong with it?" I ask.

The jockey finally calms Sleepwalker down.

"See, it's fine," my father says, puffing on his cigar. I feel like crushing it in his face. Raymond's entire college education is on this race.

"Just a little excited," my father says, as Sleepwalker totally relaxes.

The bell sounds!

"And there they go!" the announcer shouts. "Sleepwalker stumbles at the break!"

The goddamn animal gets caught in the gate.

"Jesus Christ!" I yell, gripping the railing.

My grandfather screams, "Retarded. Retarded!"

A long second later, Sleepwalker clears the gate and takes off.

"It's Floor Waxer to the front on the inside by one, Barefoot Dancer by three, Ginger Place, Little Daniel, and Sleepwalker trails the field. . . . Around the clubhouse turn, it's Floor Waxer in front by a head . . . Barefoot Dancer by three-quarters, Ginger Place by two, Little Daniel by five, and Sleepwalker trails the field . . ."

I'm gripping the railing so hard I get a splinter under my thumbnail. I look at Nathan. He's staring so intently he looks frozen. I look at my father. Somehow he's still looking cool.

"Entering the back stretch, it's Floor

Waxer in front by a head, Barefoot Dancer by two, Ginger Place by a head, Little Daniel and . . . Sleepwalker. . . . As they approach the half mile, it's Floor Waxer in front by a nose, Barefoot Dancer by a quarter, Ginger Place by one, Little Daniel, and . . . Sleepwalker still trails the field."

I peer at the old man again. He's still calm and watching through his worn binoculars. Trying to get the splinter out, I've chewed away most of my thumbnail.

"Around the far turn, it's Floor Waxer in front by a head, Barefoot Dancer by three-quarters, Ginger Place, Little Daniel by five . . . and here comes Sleepwalker drivin' on the outside . . ."

I spit out the hangnail. Me and Nathan stare at each other. I can't believe it, the goddamn horse is pulling up!

"As they enter the back stretch, it's . . . Sleepwalker now in front by a head, Floor Waxer second by two . . ."

I can't believe my eyes! And the jockey is not even whipping him!! Not even realizing it, I bite off my pinky nail.

"Into the back stretch, Sleepwalker's drawin' clear. Now it's Sleepwalker by a neck . . ."

The horse is really pulling out. My nail gets caught between my bottom front teeth but I don't even notice 'cause I'm yelling! WE'RE GOIN' CRAZY! WE'RE JUMPIN' UP AND DOWN! MY FATHER'S GONNA BE RICH! WE'RE ALL RICH! HE FINALLY DID IT. I HUG HIM. I ALMOST EVEN KISS HIM!

The track announcer seems as shocked as everybody else.

"It's Sleepwalker comin' on into the stretch. It's Floor Waxer movin' up on Sleepwalker..."

The other animal's catching up!

"It's Sleepwalker, bumping, they're bumping, nose and nose. There goes Sleepwalker drawin' out by one, by two, by three, by four—Oh God...

I will never forget what happened next. The image will probably stay with me for the rest of my life. It will be a recurring nightmare!

The goddamn animal suddenly jumps, actually jumps, over the inside fence, *and begins bucking like a wild bronco!*

I've never taken LSD, but I feel like I'm on it... I just stand there, frozen. We all do. The animal is going insane. Jumping, bucking, snorting, sneezing. The shocked jockey leaps off just in time as the frenzied animal rolls over onto his back! It gets up again and broncs up and down, up and down, like a horse gone mad...

My father's behind the wheel as we drive down the Parkway in silence. None of us has said one word... Finally I turn to Nathan, who's in the middle.

"What happened?"

He doesn't meet my eyes.

"They juiced him too much," he guesses, quietly.

This really makes me sick. Juiced means they overdosed the horse with amphetamines. I didn't know they did this anymore. I thought all races these days were fixed by paying off jockeys. I never thought that's how this race was gonna be rigged.

"Druggin' a horse," I mutter. "Those goddamn animals that do the drugging, *they* oughta be drugged. Permanently." With my left thumbnails I try to loosen the pinky nail that's still lodged between my bottom two front teeth.

My father throws his cigar stub out the window. "Half the housewives in Jersey are stoned on diet pills every day, and you're worryin' about a goddamn nag!"

"That's right," I snap.

"Then join the cavalry."

"Shuddup!" I shout.

He reaches over and smacks me. "I'm your father and I don't care what we're talkin' about. You don't talk to me like that."

I can't help laughing.

"What's so funny?" he snorts.

"A man blows two thousand seven hundred dollars, his son's entire college education—and he wants respect!"

"The subject is closed," he orders.

Now Nathan laughs sarcastically. "You think you're Napoleon?"

"I don't wanna talk about it anymore," my father says with finality.

I flip on the radio. My father turns it off.

"No music, I gotta headache."

"Well, I don't!" I say and I turn it back on.

He flicks it off again. "No music, it's my van!"

"It belongs to the business," Nathan says angrily, reaching for the knob.

"My business," Frank says, grabbing Nate's wrist.

"All of a sudden you want it!" Nathan screams.

Frank pulls off Nathan's hand and elbows him into me. Angry, I reach over and switch the radio back on. He switches it back off. I grab the dial, turn the radio on full blast, yank off the knob, and throw the knob out the window.

"Keep your eyes on the goddamn road," Nate yells as Frank reaches over and slaps me.

I lean over and slap him back harder.

My father yanks the van over to the shoulder of the road and *throws a punch. It's war. We go wild.* Cursing and punching.

Nathan, who's caught in the middle, is screaming. "Stop it, you idiots!"

By mistake, his head gets in the way of my fist. His glasses fly into the windshield and he slumps forward.

"You alright?" My old man and I ask the question together.

Nathan throws my arm off and gropes for his glasses.

My father reaches over, opens my door and pushes me out with his foot. A second later, the van peels out.

I get to my feet, and watch it swerve through traffic and then barrel down the turnpike. The back of my neck is on fire. You could light a cigarette off it. I kick an empty can of Pabst Blue Ribbon. . . . What can I do? . . . I start walking.

I'm still walking down the parkway, still kicking that Pabst Blue Ribbon beer can and still trying to get that pinky nail out, when I hear this mad honking. I look up and the van's coming from the opposite direction. *Bam!* It jumps the divider, whirls around and rockets toward me! I grab a rock and prepare myself to do battle to the end. The dry cleaning van screeches to a halt in front of me and one look at Raymond is all I need. He's sitting between Nathan and Frank and his face looks like a raw hamburger.

"Johnny De Soto?"

My brother nods, I climb in, and my father passes every single car on the road. I finally get that nail loose and spit it out angrily.

CHAPTER ELEVEN

WITH RAYMOND SQUEEZED IN NEXT TO ME IN THE van, blood from his nose dripping on his shoulder, I try to image what's going on in the Warriors' clubhouse, a shack on an abandoned pier alongside the Hudson. Johnny De Soto, I figure, is throwing his switchblade into a dart board he stole from Korvette's.

Two of the other three Warriors are playing poker with a marked deck they sent away for through a mail catalogue, and the fourth one, a slime who calls himself "Never," is drinking malt liquor by the window and watching a tugboat pull a rotted barge down the river.

The van screeches to a halt in front of the clubhouse and we all pile out. I run up to the door and shoulder it full force. It doesn't break in like in the movies. Before I can try again, my father and Nathan smash into me from behind, knocking my forehead into the door! Any other time I would've started yelling. My head is already bleeding and throbbing and I'm not inside the shack yet.

We back up a few steps and me and the old man try again. This time the door breaks in.

I'm on top of Johnny in a second! He whirls around with the blade in his hand, but I grab his wrist and bend it to the floor. It's a great defense move. Ronnie, the cop, showed it to me when I was in high school. I slap Johnny across the face and throw him against the wall.

Johnny is big—bigger than Pinky. He has big shoulders and swollen knuckles. He's a greasing hulk, but a punk just the same. I feel like ripping the earring out of his left ear, but I just smack him back and forth instead.

"You're a punk, ya hear me? You're a punk! Say it," I yell at him as I slap him back and forth without stopping. "Say it!" I'm giving him no chance. My left hand is pinned around his throat like a horseshoe. He can't move. "Say it!" I grab his nose and turn it like the handle on a vending machine.

"I'm a punk, I'm a punk!" he squeals, hurting badly.

Meanwhile, my father, with a garbage can lid he grabbed from outside, has banged the other two Warriors to the floor. And Raymond, with Nathan, has cornered Never with the baseball bat.

I let go of Johnny after he yells, "I'm a

punk!" for the tenth time. Nathan comes up behind me as Johnny slides to the floor.

"Blacken his eyes!" Nathan yells.

"It's enough!" I scream.

But Nathan crouches down next to Johnny's beet-red face, grabs the switchblade off the floor and holds it over Johnny's heart.

"No, Dad!" Frank yells, scared.

Nathan snarls at Johnny. "Ever breathe on my grandson again, I'll cut your heart out and eat it."

Satisfied, Nathan rises and we follow him out the door, leaving a wrecked clubhouse behind.

A second later, Raymond walks back inside, looks at Johnny, spits on the floor, and walks out, proud . . .

CHAPTER TWELVE

It's night and we're all down by the Hudson. This is the place where I come a lot, skip stones and think. To me, skipping stones is like a head massage.

I'm standing on the embankment. The water's twenty feet below and I can look across the river and see the New York skyline with all the bright lights.

My old man, my brother and my grandfather are behind me, slumped on an abandoned bus bench. We haven't said a word to each other, none of us, since we came from the clubhouse.

Frank is swigging from a half gallon of dark wine. The moon is high in the sky.

He takes a swig and mutters, without looking at Raymond.

"Yeah, right over there is where I was born." He points to a smoky oil refinery. "I grew up in a house usta be where that refinery is." He looks at Nathan. "Remember?"

Nathan is slumped in a deep sleep at the end of the bench.

"Can I have another sip?" Raymond says, reaching for the wine.

My father pours a gulpful into Raymond's mouth.

"I didn't get any," Raymond lies, drawing the back of his hand across his mouth, then wiping the sticky liquid off on his dungarees.

My father doesn't hear him.

"There was a whole neighborhood here, woods too. Your grandfather built me a great treehouse," my father says.

From out of nowhere, Raymond asks, "You miss Mom?"

My father looks at Raymond. A wave of loneliness passes through his body, requiring a very long gulp of wine. After a moment, he answers.

"At times."

"When do you most?" Raymond asks, staring at my father and noticing for the first time the deep crow's feet on the sides of my father's eyes.

My father thinks it over. A strange smile crosses his face as his eyes blur to a memory.

"When I hear a vacuum cleaner. It's weird, but I used to love to sit in a chair and watch your mother vacuum . . ." He takes another gulp. "Now whenever I hear a vacuum, I get the strangest chill . . ."

Raymond takes the wine out of my father's hands and drinks. My father lets him, his mind's with my mother. It's been twenty-one months since she died, and I don't think my father's stopped loving her for a moment. Somehow, too, I don't think he's accepted the fact that she's gone. Pictures of him and Mom are still all over his room, and though he gave away all of my mother's clothes after she died, he still keeps her favorite red sweater in his bottom drawer. And my mother's coffee cup is still in the kitchen cabinet. No one's ever said anything about this. We've all had our own coffee mugs for years and my mother's still sits on the third shelf. No one's ever used it, or mentioned it . . . maybe that says something about the rest of us, too.

Sure, Helen's his girlfriend, but that's all she is. It's companionship for him. When my father told Helen she'd look good as a blonde, she didn't understand, but I did.

See . . . my mother had blond hair.

My father's watching me skip stones across the Hudson. Raymond reaches down, scoops up a handful of stones and places them in his hands. My father looks at his youngest son and smiles.

"You're a good kid, smart."

He walks down to the embankment. I continue to throw the stones. He starts throwing. We don't say a word to each other, or look at each other. We just skip stones.

Before long, we're competing.

"Three skips," he says.

I fling one harder.

"Four," I say.

"Five," he says, throwing another. "See that? Five."

It takes me two more throws, but I match his best shot.

Then I hear him ask, in a very strange tone, "Think there's gates around heaven?"

I look at him and know where his mind has been. I turn back to the water and fling a stone.

"If He don't let you in, you just let me know."

He looks at me, then throws a rock straight into the water. It makes a nice *kerplunk*.

"And what would you do?"

"Whatever it took. 'Cause you two were great together."

We look at each other, and a strange, sad anger is communicated. I fling a rock straight into the water.

He finds a bigger one and heaves it.

I rip a small boulder from the earth with my hands. I wind back. I shot-put it and it makes a nice splash.

Frank moves to a huge shore boulder the size of a kitchen table. He wraps his thick arms around it and pulls with all his might.

I walk over. I brace my back and we both strain. We yank and we pull. The veins are bulging from our necks as we pull and pull. Finally it loosens. We tug at it with all our might and the boulder breaks the ground and comes loose.

We roll it over to the edge of the em-bankment.

We look at each other.

We push it off.

It sails through the air.

Splash. The splash is enormous. It's won-derful and loud. We savor each ring as it spreads noiselessly in the water.

Frank drapes his arm around my shoul-der. I wrap my arm around his and we walk back to the bench. My grandfather's arm is pro-tectively snuggled around Raymond, whose head is nestled into his chest. Both are asleep.

My old man looks at me, remembers something, then reaches into his jacket and digs out String's teeth. He looks out over the Hudson and then back at me.

"It's up to you," he says.

Both of us laugh at the same time.

And, as I'm laughing, I look up at the moon . . . and wonder what she's doing.

CHAPTER THIRTEEN

WEEKS LATER, ROSEMARIE DESCRIBED TO ME WHAT turned out to be the turning point in her life.

She's in her bedroom, which is decorated in shades of light blue. Long silk scarves hang over a chair and she's sitting up in bed, reading the biography of Isadora Duncan, a famous English dancer. She's reading the same paragraph for the third time because she can't concentrate. She's thinking of me.

You see, for a year and a half she's been going out with this guy named Scott Gunther. They met a week after Rosemarie and her mother moved to Hoboken from Bellevue two years ago. Rosemarie got the job teaching at the deaf school, one of only six in New Jersey, and her mother opened up her own real estate office in

East Rutherford, not too far from Hoboken. They hadn't planned to move here. Mrs. Lemon wanted to live closer to East Rutherford, but she got a great buy on a house from one of her clients who was strapped for cash, so she grabbed it.

Her parents got divorced when Rosemarie was fourteen. Her father, who sold office supplies, met a younger woman at a convention in Miami. A year later Rosemarie's parents were legally divorced, and Mrs. Lemon went into the real estate business. Rosemarie and her mother are very close, and as I came to learn later, have a lot in common. Mrs. Lemon was once a dancer with the Rockettes. Matter of fact, that's how she met her husband. He came to see a show at Radio City Music Hall, then went backstage, and within eighteen months they were married.

Anyway, on that fateful afternoon, Rosemarie closes the book and thinks about Scott again. Rudy, her cat, rubs against her elbow, wanting her to stroke him. Scott is intelligent, attractive, kind and generous, she thinks to herself, massaging the cat's tiny ears. When he learned that Rosemarie loved dance, he read articles about ballet and took her to see Nureyev in New York. He was also active in the deaf movement. Deaf movement? Oh, yeah, Women's Liberation, Black Liberation, Gay Liberation . . . Deaf Liberation is next. Most of the people involved in this movement come from Gallaudet, the college for the deaf in Washington, D. C. Scott graduated from Gallaudet. Like he says to Rosemarie, Bob Hope tells a joke on TV, but there are no captions. Do the networks think the deaf don't like to laugh? More TV programs should be captioned, not just the news, and Scott is one of those responsible for putting pressure on local stations to do so . . .

He's a good man, Rosemarie thinks. And he does love me. So why . . . why can't I love him back?

She pulls the quilt off her legs, walks over to the window and stares out . . . She watches the lights of a jet plane passing overhead in the sky and wonders where it's headed and who's on it.

Then a thought passes through her mind. Scott's been asking her to go away for a weekend. A long drive up to Boston. He'd like her to meet his friends who perform in the National Theatre of the Deaf, which is located in Boston. They could see a dress rehearsal of a new play the company is planning to open Christmas weekend. It sounds like a very pleasant weekend, which is exactly why Rosemarie doesn't want to go. Everything with Scott is pleasant. Dating is pleasant. Kissing him is pleasant. Sex with Scott is pleasant.

That's just the problem.

CHAPTER FOURTEEN

I'M WAITING FOR ROSEMARIE IN FRONT OF HER school as the bus pulls up. A lot of people get off, but no Rosemarie. The bus pulls away and then I see her. She's riding in the passenger seat of a new Pinto, which pulls up and parks in front of the school, not far from where I am.

Rosemarie and Scott Gunther climb out. He looks like a teacher. He's handsome, blond, he wears a tie and he's got a flesh-colored hearing aid in his left ear.

As they walk up to the school, she sees me. She's surprised and she even looks happy to see me. With a flurry of his hands, Scott asks her who I am. I get that much. She's looking at me and she doesn't see his question. Then she turns to him and signs. She tells him, I think, that she'll meet him inside.

He heads toward the school, not happy, as she walks over to me. I decide not to ask her about him. I don't want to know.

"Hi, how are you?" I say slowly.

She looks at me and nods.

"I was driving by the neighborhood, see? There's my van." I point to it. "My family owns a dry cleaner's."

She looks at the van, and back at me. She seems to be studying my face.

"So I thought I'd stop by and say hello. Hello."

She signs hello. At least, I guess that's what she's signing. Then she points toward the school and starts walking.

"Also, I wanted to ask . . ." I step in front of her. "Would you like to go out Saturday night?" The words come out very fast.

She looks at me and shakes her head.

I'm walking backwards in front of her as she's walking forward. I'm going to get a date with this girl. I'm determined. "You can't? How about Friday night? No?" She tries to step around me. I stay with her.

"Saturday? How about during the day? We can have coffee? No? How about I just come over and visit you at your home for a little while?"

She doesn't answer. I'm thinking that she wants to say yes, but she won't. I can feel it. There's something in her eyes that makes me believe this.

120

"All right, I'll tell you what. I'll just come over, ring the bell and leave."

I get a smile.

We're now at the door to the school and all the kids are waiting for her. Cheryl, the little black girl, as usual is off to the side, away from the others. I smile at her. She grins back at me. Rosemarie notices this as I turn back to her. "About noon? Is that a good time?" I ask. "I'll come over and ring the bell. Look, if you want to open the door, you will, if you don't, you won't."

She looks at me. Up close, she's got the most beautiful pale blue eyes I've ever seen in my life. And skin like silk, which is framed by her light brown hair. Actually she isn't gorgeous beautiful which maybe I've made her sound like. I mean, she's not *Playmate* centerfold beautiful or model beautiful . . . Rosemarie is just . . . simply beautiful.

I'm still waiting for her answer as I stare into her eyes. She nods and a thrill goes through my body. I whip out a pencil and paper, one from each pocket, like a gunfighter.

She writes down her address, then disappears inside the building.

It's later in the day as I pull my van up in front of the Stanley Theatre. I climb out with an armload of dry-cleaned uniforms. We service this place. I slip the parking ticket under the windshield and amble inside.

All I can think about is Rosemarie.

The theatre's closed. There's no matinee

today. It's empty except for an old black mainte-nance man who's on top of a ladder cleaning the chandelier. On the back of his shirt is EASTERN MAINTENANCE COMPANY. I know the place. They used to service our store. Wax the floors once a month. That is, they did until my father got into an argument with the owner and stopped paying their bills.

What was the argument about? I asked him a few months ago. He's not even sure. Two months later, he bought a hot floor waxing machine from String who got it from who knows where. He said he was going to do the floor waxing himself and save money. He's used it exactly once since then. It's been eight months since the floors have been done in the shop. If I have nothing else to do this weekend, maybe I'll do them.

I yell up to the maintenance man. "Is the manager around?"

"Yeah, around the corner having coffee! Want to leave those?"

"I gotta get paid."

"He'll be back in a few minutes."

I nod and wander inside the theatre. The Stanley is the second largest movie theatre in the country. It holds something like three thousand five hundred people. The place is immense. Three balconies.

I walk down the aisle and look up at the screen. Suddenly I see Rosemarie's face, forty feet high! She looks just the way she looked when I first saw her in the train station. She's looking at me and smiling like she did this morning.

I sink down into an aisle seat and let my mind go. I turn around in my seat and look around the empty theatre. Suddenly, it's filled. I look back at the stage and it's rising slowly and I'm on it, dressed in a white suit with my light blue, spread-collar shirt. The band is behind me. The theatre is packed. Rosemarie's sitting in the front row, and I'm singing my song to her. I'm a big hit and the people are loving me. I'm singing this song, a special fantasy song I wrote one Saturday morning down by the Hudson. It's called "On the Stage." It goes like this.

> *I've been waiting all of my life*
> *To be here tonight,*
> *To stand in this light*
> *Shining this bright*
>
> *I've been waiting all of my life*
> *To turn a new page*
> *Out of my cage*
> *Now I'm coming of age . . .*

The drums come in. Petey never sounded better. And suddenly, as we break into the chorus, I have a full orchestra behind me!

> *On a stage*
> *I know my life is something real*
> *On a stage*
> *There are no words for what I feel*
> *For I can heal the emptiness on a stage.*

VOICES

I've been standing all of my life
Outside the parade
Lonely charade,
Lost in the shade.

All of my life,
The city's tried to get me to crawl
Make me feel small
But I'm forty feet tall!

When I'm on a stage ...
I know my life is something real
On a stage
There are no words for what I feel
For I reveal
The man I really am
On a stage ... On a stage ... On a
stage ... !!

Later that day, I'm no longer in my
fantasy, but I'm singing just the same. Me and
the band are just finishing our audition in front
of Mr. Patterson and we never sounded better,
especially Fred on the sax. There are other bands
waiting to audition, but I tell you we're hot like
I said we'd be.

Patterson is sitting at a table. Pinky's
standing alongside. He's watching his boss for
his reaction. As I'm singing, Pinky waves at me,
trying to get my attention. I look over at him and
he yawns, big. But I notice Patterson's tapping
his foot.

124

The song ends and Patterson turns to Pinky.

Pinky scowls. "Personally, I think he's got nothing, Mr. Patterson. The band's all right, but what's his name stinks!" He adjusts the cufflink on his right sleeve.

Patterson smiles. He understands. "Ever wanted to be a singer, Louis?" he asks, sipping a brandy.

"Excuse me?" Pinky's head jerks.

Patterson nods toward Ned and Racer. Ned, as I told you before, is Mr. Patterson's personal bodyguard and the bouncer for the restaurant. Racer is Mr. Patterson's chauffeur. He's a thin man, about fifty-five, with long sideburns.

"Take Ned and Racer into the kitchen. Have Leonard give them whatever they want."

Pinky defends himself. "I never wanted to be a singer, Mr. Patterson, I just gave you my opinion."

As I walk up to the table, Patterson dismisses Pinky with a wave of the hand.

"Tell them to try the steamers, Louis."

Pinky boils inside. Being dismissed in front of me is enormously insulting.

"You and your band have material?" Patterson asks. He notices my chewed-down fingernails, then looks at his own, probably reminding himself it's time for another manicure.

"For costumes?"

"Songs—hits," he laughs. "Do you know many?"

"All of them," I tell him, self-consciously tucking my fingers under my hand, knowing he's staring at them, and feeling a little embarrassed because I don't usually bite my nails. It's just that during that horse race I did a lot of things I don't usually do, like hug my father.

The phone rings by the register, and a second later Pinky comes over.

"Telephone call from an agent named Meier who wants to send us a great new up and coming band. I heard 'em once in Passaic an' they're going to be big. I told them five o'clock today. Is that okay, Mr. Patterson?"

Patterson looks me over for a second and then turns back to Pinky.

"We have a band."

I'm thrilled inside. The guys in the band hear the news and are quietly jubilant.

The news is poison for Pinky. Envy swells through his body and I'll bet anything he broke out that night.

CHAPTER FIFTEEN

I'M IN MY BEDROOM WITH THE BOOK IN FRONT OF me. I got it propped up open on my dresser. I'm trying to learn some of the stuff and it's not really hard.

"Good morning, good afternoon, good night. Place the tips of the open hand against the mouth and throw them forward."

I try it. "Good night. Good night."

I look in the mirror and try it again. "Good night. Good night." The title of the book is *Talk to the Deaf*. The cover says, "A practical visual guide, useful to anyone wishing to master sign language and the manual alphabet."

I went to the library after the audition. Rather, I flew to the library. I was grinning from ear to ear. I had a real job. No topless dancer jiggling alongside me. It's now just me and the Jersey Turnpike doing what we love to do. Playing music. The money's not great but it's not bad and this is a real beginning. Montrose Meier wanted to send over a great new up and coming group from Passaic, Pinky said. No doubt Johnny "Filet Mignon" Newark was their lead singer. But Mr. Patterson bought hamburger instead!

So now I'm studying the book so I can surprise Rosemarie. On each page, there are illustrations of hands making word signs used by the deaf, accompanied by an explanation.

I thumb through the word index, looking for "coffee." I find it and turn to page 124.

"Coffee—Place the right fist over the left fist and make a counter-clockwise grinding motion."

I make the sign. Then I find the word "is."

"Is—Place the tip of the index finger at the mouth and move it forward, still upright."

"The coffee is . . ."

I have the beginning of my sentence.

I want to say "delicious." I go through the index but there is no listing for "delicious."

" 'Great', how about 'great'," I mutter to myself. But the word "great" is not listed either. At least you don't have to learn a million words in this language.

I settle on "good." I turn to the page which gives the sign.

"Good—Touch the lips with the fingers of the right hand and then move the right hand forward placing it palm up into the palm of the left hand."

I do the sign, then put them all together: "The coffee is good."

I turn to the mirror and watch myself. "The coffee is good, the coffee is good." I had already learned to say, "How was your day?" so now I had the beginnings of a conversation.

"The coffee is good. How was your day? The coffee is good, how was your day?"

The bedroom door opens behind me. I slip the book into the dresser drawer and spin around.

"Who're you talking to?" Raymond asks, blowing a bubble which pops and splatters over his mouth.

"What do you mean?"

"You were talking to somebody," he says, looking around the room, licking the gum off his face.

"Just, uh, working on a song, trying to write one myself."

"The coffee is good, how was your day?" he says, pushing the gum with his finger from the sides of his mouth back inside.

"Yeah, catchy lyrics. Don't you think everybody can relate to those words?"

"Sure, Drew. Top of the chart."

I start to sing: "The coffee is good, how was your day? The coffee is good, how was your day?"

Raymond looks at me strangely, blowing another bubble which again splatters all over his mouth.

CHAPTER SIXTEEN

It's Saturday afternoon and six minutes to one as I pull up in front of Rosemarie's house.

She really lives in a house, not an apartment like me. Nice neighborhood, too. She lives on the north side of Hoboken, in the hills.

I'm wearing a turtleneck and I'm feeling very snappy, as I amble up to the door. In my hand I got a rose, a long-stemmed red rose I bought from Juan the florist on Fourth Street.

I pause at the door and I practice the signs:

"The coffee is good. How was your day?" I pass my test and, satisfied, press the bell.

Rosemarie opens the door, and my God, she's looking terrific. She's got her hair down, she's wearing an open-necked white blouse with an Indian print vest and a beige skirt.

I love women in skirts and dresses. It's feminine, which I think a woman should be. The main reason I'm really attracted to Rosemarie is . . . she's got class. Style. She's a lady.

"How did you hear the doorbell?" I ask. 'Cause I didn't hear anything.

She sticks her hand outside and presses it. I see the lights flash on and off and I grin.

"Hey, that's pretty smart," I say, making sure my lips don't move too fast.

She smiles.

I enter. I look around and I'm impressed. The house is tastefully furnished. They live comfortably. They're not rich but they're well off.

"Hey, nice place." I pull the rose out from behind my back. "Rose—Marie."

She smiles and mouths the words, "thank you," as she signs them.

I follow her into the kitchen, and as she places the rose in a vase and fills it with water, I notice perking coffee.

"Ahhhh—coffee!"

She gestures to it, asking me if I'd like some. I nod and take a seat at the kitchen table. The cat jumps up on the table, as I notice a stack of *Dance* magazines on the windowsill.

"Who's this?" I ask her. Her back's to me so she doesn't hear. As she turns, I say again, "Who's this?"

She smiles, comes over and takes the cat off the table and drops it on the floor.

"Pretty cat," I say, and again, she's not looking at me and she misses that as well. She turns back to the coffee and I don't repeat myself. The cat jumps back on the table. I pet it and then put it back on the floor.

All of a sudden the kitchen lights start flashing on and off. I look to the front door, but Rosemarie walks into the living room, to a phone on a table. It's some kind of special typewriter-like phone. I watch, intrigued, as she takes the receiver off the hook and places it in a holder. All of a sudden the machine starts typing by itself! I found out later it was that teacher, Scott, calling to ask her out.

"Hi. It's me. Want to see a movie tonight?"

She types back, "Hi, Scott. No I can't. Thanks anyway. I'm busy right now. I'll call you later. Bye."

The machine types back, "Bye," then Rosemarie replaces the phone and returns to the coffee in the kitchen.

I make the brilliant comment, "That's a great idea." And once again—I still haven't learned—she doesn't hear me.

She comes over to the table and pours the coffee. I can't wait to surprise her with my compliment. I pick up the cup and sip it, scalding my tongue!

"Agghh!"

She fills a glass with water from the sink. I gulp it down, then feel like killing myself.

No one can embarrass me better than I can myself. Once I saw Frankie Valli in the

Tavern restaurant in Newark. I walked over and told him I was a fan, which I was, and he invited me to sit down. I ordered a beer and asked him how he got started. It's a fascinating story, actually, how he got together with the Four Seasons, how they recorded "Sherry," how "The Lion Sleeps Tonight" came about. As I'm leaning forward listening—I was only nineteen and here I was drinking beer with Frankie Valli—I picked up the frosty mug and . . . missed my mouth completely. Down my chin and all over my shirt it went!

That night I had a dream I was having lobster with Frank Sinatra at Hoboken's Famous Clam House. As the waitress put the lobster down in front of me, Frank, who had just heard me sing, was telling me what a giant star I was gonna be and how he wanted to take me back to Vegas with him. I'm nodding, "Yes, yes," dunking a large forkful of lobster into a sauce of melted butter. Then as Frank asks if twenty-five thousand a week is all right for openers, I stick the dripping piece of lobster in my eye!

Both of these memories flash through my mind in the two seconds it takes me to drink the water.

Rosemarie takes a seat and I smile, trying to clear my mind of what I was just remembering. A few seconds of pregnant silence pass. Then I carefully take a tiny sip. I look up at her and *boom!* My mind's a blank, I can't remember the signs! I can't remember anything, not even the word "the." What's wrong? her eyes say.

Just as fast it all comes back.

I point to the coffee and make a grinding motion with one fist over the other. I push my upright index finger away from my mouth, then I touch my lips with my right hand and place it in the open palm of my left ...

She's touched! I shrug it off, then look around casually and ask: "You live alone in this big place?"

The house really is roomy, at least compared to my place it is. Must be great growing up in a house with a backyard. Take it from me, growing up in an apartment stinks. Well, maybe it's not that bad, but every time I go visit somebody in a house it just makes me realize how much I wanna bring up my family in a house. I want privacy, that's what I want, privacy. I don't want my kids growing up like I did hearing arguments through the next wall.

One other girl I dated lived in a house something like this. Her name was Caroline. We went out for six years from when I was 16 to 22. She had a twin sister, Linda, but they were nothing alike. I guess Caroline was the only girl I think I've ever loved. What happened was simple: we just grew away from each other. Not physically, emotionally. We were always great together physically ... sexually, I mean. I could never get enough of her. I swear, sometimes when I was kissing her, I wanted to swallow her.

We had a lotta great times together. Caroline was a year younger than me. The thing was she went to college and I didn't. She commuted to Seton Hall in South Orange, and down there she met a whole group of different people.

She got into smoking grass which I could never get into, and one Christmas vacation she came home and told me she had tripped. I couldn't believe it. She came home wearing beads that week. She had also repierced her left earlobe a second time and was now wearing two earrings in it.

"Don't knock it until you try it. Don't be so closed . . . Open yourself to new things . . . Don't be so old fashioned." That's all she seemed to be saying to me that Christmas vacation. It was the beginning of the end. After her spring vacation, we stopped seeing each other.

That summer she went to Europe. She dropped me two postcards—one from Amsterdam and the other from Marrakesh, Morocco. I didn't even know where Morocco was, I had to look on the map. It's in North Africa. She laughingly joked she had spent the night in jail there. The guy she was traveling with had been picked up for carrying *kief*—some kind of African grass. Caroline stayed in Europe instead of coming back to college for her fall semester. After she'd been home a week she gave me a call.

The day after Thanksgiving we met on the hill where Aaron Burr and Hamilton shot at each other. We used to go there and make out when we were in high school. I can't tell you how strange it was seeing her again. It was like I didn't know who she was. There was none of the old Caroline left in her. Her eyes were still the same beautiful greenish hazel, her hair was still blond and straight. Her body even looked the same except these days she didn't wear a bra. But she, Caroline, was another person. I told her how I'd definitely decided to quit the brewery and try and make it as a singer. She said, "Far out."

I hummed her a new song I was writing. She said, "Groovy, I really dig it. It's far out, man, far out."

The word "man" is what really threw me. Her calling me "man" and not Drew turned me off. I told her, "Don't call me 'man', my name is Drew." She said, "All right, hey, sure, don't let it get you uptight."

We made love that night—why, I don't know. In spite of the enormous gap between us, I guess we wanted to see if there was anything still there. I've never enjoyed making love less. As a matter of fact, it wasn't making love, it was like going through a motion. We both pretended, we made sounds and breathed heavy—but there was nothing there.

I drove her home that night, walked her to her door and I said goodbye. She wished me luck, and I haven't seen her since. A friend of hers I ran into told me she's living in San Francisco and is into astral projection, whatever the hell that is.

At that moment a car pulls up in the driveway outside and a lady steps out with a bag full of groceries.

Rosemarie opens the front door as her mother enters. Right away it's obvious where Rosemarie got her looks. Mrs. Lemon is in her early fifties and still an attractive woman. Yet there's a certain hardness in her face. I make a correct guess that Rosemarie's father is no longer around. Later she tells me her parents are divorced.

Rosemarie takes the groceries from her mother and sets them on the counter. She points to me and does some sign language. Her mother nods to me.

"I'm Rosemarie's mother," she says, very slowly, mouthing the words.

I stand up politely and extend my open hand.

"Drew Rothman. It's a pleasure."

She's very surprised.

"You can hear me!"

"Oh, I'm not deaf."

Immediately she regards me suspiciously.

"Then you don't teach at the school?"

"No, I'm a singer, Mrs. Lemon."

"You're a singer?" She looks down at my boots which I polished but are old and need new heels.

"Where do you sing?" she asks, as she raises her eyes to my leather jacket with notable distaste.

"Uh, well, looks like I'll be working in a new disco soon." I smile, which is not easy because I can feel the bad vibes.

"Oh . . . where have you sung before?" she asks, starting to take the groceries out of the bag and trying to be casual which I doubt she could ever be.

"Uhh . . . different places. Around."

I'm not gonna tell her I've been working

in a topless joint. If I did, I think she'd call the police.

She measures me with great skepticism, looks at Rosemarie, then back at me.

"In between jobs I work for my father, Rothman Dry Cleaners, down on Hamilton Avenue. Do you know it?"

"No."

"I do pick-up and deliveries. But it's only till the career gets rolling."

Rosemarie asks her mother something with her hands. Mrs. Lemon looks up at me as she signs: "He was just telling me that he's a delivery boy for a dry cleaner and he wants to be a singer."

"No," I corrected her, "I am a singer."

She looks at me with a tight smile.

"No reason to become upset, Mr. Rothman."

"Did I say something to offend you?" I ask.

She looks innocently at Rosemarie, as if she's confused. "Why, no." Then she swivels her position in such a way that Rosemarie can't see what she's saying.

"Have you met Rosemarie's boyfriend? Scott's almost totally deaf but he plays the harmonica."

Rosemarie turns her mother around and signs at her angrily.

"What are you saying, Rosemarie?"

Rosemarie looks at her mother a moment, then walks straight over to the coat rack, takes my coat off and hands it to me.

"You want me to go?" I ask.

She nods, and a satisfied look crosses her mother's face.

Very disappointed, I head for the door.

Rosemarie opens it, grabs her sweater off a hook and exits with me.

We walk out to the porch and I'm smiling. I open the door for her.

We climb into the dry cleaning van and drive off. Communicating is very, very difficult. I only know two sentences in sign, and I'm not about to ask her how her day was. Plus I can't look at her and talk slowly as I drive. So we don't say anything for the first ten minutes. Then, as I pull up to a street light on the corner of Hamilton Avenue, I turn to her and say, very slowly, "Rosemarie, just how much of what I say do you get from reading my lips?"

She mouths the word, "Half."

Half, I think to myself as the light turns green and I drive through the intersection which is pitted badly and needs repaving. My God, what a different world she lives in, and I'll bet anything she's thinking the same thing about me.

At the next light I turn to her and ask, "Are you hungry?" I mime "eating," which I find out later is the correct sign. As a matter of fact, a lotta signs for the deaf are what you might think up naturally.

She nods and I drive over to Solly's, a Jewish delicatessen I've been going to since I'm a kid.

I park outside, walk around the van, open the door for her and we go inside.

Jack, the owner, who bought the place from a guy named Solly, who moved to Miami and started a beach chair rental business, is behind the counter. He looks up and smiles at me.

"Hi, Drew!"

"Hiya, Jack. How's the brisket?"

"All gone."

"No."

His wife, Julie, a thin woman with a heavily lined face, shakes her head and laughs.

"He's just kiddin', Drew, we have plenty."

I shoot Jack a look, he grins and nods toward Rosemarie, impressed.

Debbie, the shapely waitress, ambles over to me with a sly grin on her face.

"Drew. Haven't seen you around," she says, looking over Rosemarie.

"Hi, Debbie. I've been busy."

"I can see," she remarks with a touch of sarcasm.

"All the way in the back," I ask, "in the corner. Could we have that table, Debbie?"

"Anything for you, Drew."

We follow her and I can feel Rosemarie is not feeling comfortable. Neither am I and I realize it's a big mistake, us coming here.

Debbie pulls out a chair for Rosemarie, then looks up at me with that same sly smile.

"Are you happy?"

"Yeah, this is great. Thanks."

"I haven't seen you before. Is this your first time here?" she asks Rosemarie.

Rosemarie nods, not appreciating the way she's smiling at her. Debbie waits for Rosemarie to say more. Rosemarie doesn't.

"Table's great. Thanks a lot, Debbie," I say, wanting her to leave very fast.

She gives me a look and leaves.

Rosemarie and I sit down. I open the menu and point to the sandwiches.

"Corned beef, pastrami, brisket, all these sandwiches are delicious. This place is known for them."

She nods, then looks back toward Debbie, then back to me, questioningly.

"Debbie? Oh, when I was working at the brewery—see I usta work in a brewery—Debbie worked in the accounting office."

Three men in bowling shirts at the next table are looking over at me. One turns on a portable radio which blares. Rosemarie is waiting for me to tell her more about Debbie. She knows there's a history there.

"We went out a couple of . . ." The radio is so loud I can't even hear myself. I turn to the bowlers. "Could you turn that down a little, please?" I turn back to Rosemarie.

"You ever try a Kosher hot dog?"

She twirls her hands in a backward motion, and I understand. She wants me to finish the sentence I didn't finish.

"Oh . . . Debbie. We went out a couple of times."

She nods. The guys at the next table

only lower the radio a little bit. I'm becoming aggravated. I'm about to turn back to them, when Rosemarie stops me, pulls a pen from her purse and writes on the paper placemat: "Do you want to change seats?"

I shake my head. Then she continues and writes again: "The music won't bother me."

I look at her and I think about that: the music won't bother her. Music is my life, and it won't bother her.

"No, I'm alright," I answered as Debbie arrives with a pot of coffee.

"Coffee, Drew?" she says, as she gives me that slinky look of hers.

I nod and turn over the coffee mugs sitting in front of us on the table. Debbie fills both. "You want cream?"

"Yeah."

She turns to Rosemarie. "Cream, honey?"

Rosemarie doesn't hear her, and Debbie walks away. "Rosemarie, did you want cream?"

Rosemarie looks at me, not catching what I said.

"Did you want cream?"

She shakes her head, but somehow I know she does want some.

"Look, you want some, we'll get it. Debbie!"

Rosemarie grabs my hand. The bowlers at the next table are staring at us. I'm really getting hot. I turn to them. "Hey, something bothering you guys?"

I turn back to Rosemarie. I can feel the heat at the back of my neck.

"Look, let's get outta here. You want to leave? I'm not hungry, are you?"

She shakes her head. I stand up, throw a dollar on the table and we leave fast.

The date's a total failure—a washout.

I walk Rosemarie to her door. I notice that her mother's car's not there. I pace for a second. "Well, uh, goodbye," I say, hoping she'll invite me in.

She looks at me and nods. She is feeling as tense as I am.

"How do you say 'goodbye' in sign language?" I ask. I already know how 'cause I'd looked it up last night, but I'm thinking maybe it'll break the tension.

She just shakes her head.

"What?" I don't understand.

She points to me, back to herself and just shakes her head.

"What are you saying? It won't work?"

She nods.

"Because you already got a boyfriend?"

She shakes her head, then she nods, then she shakes her head, then she just throws up her hands. She doesn't know what she wants to say, she's as confused as I am. But I know what I want so I keep on.

"Listen, I know it didn't work today. But we could try again."

She doesn't want to. She unlocks the door and enters the house.

I stand there a moment, feeling totally useless. I don't know what to do. I start to walk away but I don't want to leave. I can't leave. We gotta talk some more. I knock on the door.

I know she's right on the other side of that door. I depress the doorbell, but she doesn't answer.

Inside, the lights flash on and off, but she won't open the door. She hurries down the hall into her bedroom and slams the door.

I'm still ringing the bell. I don't know what I'm going to say to her but I just want her to let me in. I don't want to walk away, leaving her like this. Leaving myself like this . . .

CHAPTER SEVENTEEN

THE NEXT MORNING I COME OUT OF THE STORE with an armful of deliveries. I climb behind the wheel of the van, stuff my ears with cotton and start the engine. As I jam the van into first gear, Nathan hurries out with two packages of laundry. He yells, "You forgot the Schwartz delivery! Hey, Drew!" I don't hear what he's saying and I start to drive away.

"Where are you going? Hey . . ."

I pull out, and Nathan is very confused.

I deliver two tuxedos to Mister Alvarado, a retired maitre d' who still has his old uniforms cleaned every four months "to maintain them," he says, "in case he decides to return to work," which I doubt he will, because he's seventy-five. I climb back into the van, replug my ears with the cotton and again I look at the world from a silent point of view.

I want to know what it's like not to hear. I'm not giving up on Rosemarie Lemon. Korina was right—she is special even though our one date was a fiasco. This might sound stupid, but that one day and the few times I've been with her, I've also felt special.

Later in the day, as I'm driving down Main Street, I pull up to a light and do what I've been doing all afternoon. I got the book alongside me open on the seat, and I'm practicing the deaf alphabet . . . A, B, C, D, E, F. . . . Raymond is at the corner with Demetrius. The two of them are pitching old sneakers up onto the telephone wires. Everybody does this in Hoboken. I don't know how it got started, but it's just always been that way. When your sneakers get too old and ripped up to wear, you don't throw 'em out, you pitch 'em up onto the telephone wires.

Demetrius sees the van and nudges my brother. "Hey, Ray, there's your brother."

Raymond looks up and yells, "Hey, Drew. Give us a ride."

I'm practicing the alphabet in the rearview mirror, with the cotton in my ears, and I don't notice him.

Demetrius looks at Raymond. "What's he doing, learning to talk to an Indian?"

Raymond speeds up to the van. My window's down and he's only yards away when he yells again. "Drew!"

I go through the light and drive off, leaving a very bewildered brother behind.

That night, it's three o'clock in the morning and I'm under the covers, studying the book with a flashlight. My brother's watching my bundle form under the blanket. He hears me muttering.

"J. K. L. M . . ."

I pause and run through the letters again. I'm all the way up to M, and I got them down good.

The next morning I'm washing my hair in the shower, still working on the alphabet. I'm close to conquering it. "Q, R, S, T, U, V, W, X, Y, Z . . ." I lather my hair again and go through it once more. I go from A to Z and make only two mistakes. I run through it again and make no mistakes. Then I spell her name out with my left hand. ROSEMARIE. I rinse my hair with satisfaction, and at this moment, Raymond is in our bedroom holding my book in his hands, feeling very worried. He found it under my blanket.

He hurries down the hallway into the kitchen where Frank and Nathan are having breakfast.

As I'm drying my hair, the rest of them are having a very serious discussion over Raisin Bran, which they are not touching.

Frank is staring at Raymond and Nathan, with a pale face.

"You sure?" he asks Raymond and Nathan.

Nathan nods. "I told you, I called after him yesterday. I was ten feet away."

Raymond nods. "And I ran right up to the van. I was just a few feet away!"

Nathan turns to Raymond. "Show him."

149

Raymond hands my father my *Talk to the Deaf* book.

"From all that goddamn loud music every night," my father gasps.

"Or maybe when he got hit with that construction worker's car. Maybe that caused something," Nathan says, nervously.

"Drew's going deaf," Raymond mutters.

"Jesus," Frank says, low.

"What'll we do?" Raymond says, feeling scared.

I come down the hall, whistling happy.

"Shhh!" Frank says to Raymond and Nathan.

"A deaf singer?" Raymond whispers.

"Shhh!"

My old man hides the book as I enter. I take a seat and grab the Raisin Bran with a smile.

"Everybody's coming down to Patterson's Saturday night. It's opening night."

My old man, Nathan and Raymond all exchange looks.

My father turns to me.

"What time does it start?"

"Come around eight."

"They're expecting a big crowd, aren't they?" Nathan asks.

I measure him. "I'm right here."

He speaks up even louder.

"What did you say?"

"I said I'm right here. What are you yelling for?"

"Who's yellin'?"

150

"What the hell you guys screamin' at?"

My old man stares at me. *"Nobody's screaming! Ya havin' trouble with your ears?"*

"Am I havin' what?"

"TROUBLE WITH YOUR EARS," Nathan yells.

I stand up. *"I am now!"*

"THEN LET'S GET YOU TO A DOCTOR."

"FOR WHAT?"

"YOU'RE GOING DEAF," Raymond shouts.

"I'M GOIN' DEAF???"

"WE KNOW!" Frank exclaims as he slams my book on the table.

I look at the book. I realize what's happened and I burst out laughing!

They all exchange bewildered looks. My old man puts his hand on my shoulder like he hasn't done since I'm a kid and they found me in the elevator. His face is riddled with concern.

"Maybe you better lie down, Drew," he says softly.

"You guys kill me!"

Frank looks at his father. "Brain damage, too."

"I'm not deaf," I tell them as I recover from laughing. "But I'm seeing a girl who is. I met this girl. She's deaf."

"That girl we saw?" Raymond says.

"What girl?" my father snaps.

"That beautiful girl's deaf?" Raymond says, shocked.

"What girl?" my father yells, even louder.

"*Stop shoutin'*. Her name's Rosemarie Lemon."

"And she can't hear?" Frank asks, relaxing a bit.

"That's what deaf usually means, doesn't it? I plugged my ears with cotton for a couple of days to see what it's like and I got this book."

The table becomes quiet as this information sinks in.

"What happened to her? She's always been deaf?" my father asks, reaching for his coffee, which is cold.

"I don't know," I shrug, and pour Raisin Bran in the bowl.

"A deaf girl, huh? What do you talk about?"

"It's not easy. She talks, but in sign language."

"She's deaf and dumb?" Nathan asks.

"She's not dumb," I snap. "She's smarter than all of us. She's a teacher."

"You know what I mean."

"I don't like that word."

"But if she's only deaf," Raymond asks, "how come she don't . . . talk?"

I start to answer . . . then I realize I don't know the answer. For the first time, I think this over. Then I remember that day I wandered into the school's Adult Social Club and everybody had those really weird voices that made them sound retarded.

My mind whirls like a washing machine . . .

CHAPTER EIGHTEEN

I DON'T FINISH BREAKFAST. I DRIVE RIGHT OVER TO Rosemarie's school. I park out front, slip the ticket under the windshield and trot up the steps.

I hear a lot of noise coming from the gym at the end of the hall. I peer inside the door. Rosemarie's there. She's teaching her class a song in sign language. An elderly nun is playing the piano as Rosemarie sings the song with her hands and the children try to follow along. What a job she's doing. Not only is she keeping an eye on the kids but she's also keeping an eye on the nun, who's nodding and keeping rhythm with her hand, helping Rosemarie to follow along with the beat of the song.

I step inside the room. She turns and sees

me. I smile and sign, "Good morning, Rose-marie."

She looks at me. She signs back, "Good morning," then looks at the nun and nods that it's okay for me to be there.

I try to fade into the background, but all the kids are looking at me and Cheryl is giggling and swinging her legs excitedly. She yells at Rosemarie.

"Dand dalone fur ush! Dand dalone, Miss Lemon, Dand dalone fur ush." And the other kids pick it up!

"Yeah! Dand dalone!"

Cheryl comes over to me. "You wanda shee Miss Lemon dand, dond you? Dond you?"

I understand what she's saying.

"Yeah, sure," I nod.

Then all the kids surround Rosemarie and demand that she dance alone—especially Cheryl. She wants me to see Rosemarie dance.

Rosemarie nods. The whole class applauds. It's a big treat for them.

Rosemarie walks over to a table where there's a small record player and I notice a funny thing. The speakers to the record player are both on the floor, and one of them is literally turned right to the floor. As she lifts up the needle to place it on the record, she turns to me and gestures for me to hold my ears. It doesn't sink in until the record starts. The music is on full volume!

What happened next I'll never forget for the rest of my life.

Rosemarie Lemon doesn't just dance to the song on that record—she becomes that song! It was just a simple children's song, but I'll never forget it.

What she does, I learn later, is called a sign language dance. She interprets the lyrics to the song with her hands and her face and her arms and her whole body. It's an amazing sight. The words go like this:

You can swim like a fish if you want to
Swim if you're brave enough to try
And the whales will be amazed when
they see you,
In the deepest . . . ocean drifting by.

You can run like a stream if you want to
Run down the river to the sea
And the ocean will be full of envy when
she
Sees you . . . running out to me!

I'm feeling hypnotized. I can't take my eyes off her. Neither can the kids or the nun.

You can grow like a tree if you want to
Grow if you're not afraid to fall
And all the other trees will be jealous,
when they
See you . . . standing straight and tall.

You can fly like a bird if you want to
Fly like a bird if you dare

And all the other birds will admire you,
when they
See you . . . dancing in mid-air . . .

Every kid in the world, I'm thinking, should hear this song. It should be a national anthem for kids. Those simple words really hit me hard. The philosophy behind them is everything I believe in.

Believe in yourself, and you can do anything.

As she finishes her dance, I'm thinking to myself, God, this girl can't hear a word, yet she dances so beautifully, so gracefully, hardly missing a beat. I can't believe it . . . Then I realize my eyes have tears in them, and I turn away fast and wipe them.

I pick Rosemarie up at her house at eight o'clock. (We made a date before I left the school.)

We drive around for a while. I don't mention the other night and neither does she. I love the way she dresses. I don't know if I mentioned that. Eloquent, that's the word . . . not elegant, eloquent's the way she looks. Simple but eloquent.

I want to be alone with her this time, not go to some public place, so we go over to the park and just walk around. I don't ask her the question that's been pounding in my brain since breakfast. I'm gonna lead up to it slowly.

As we sit down on the swings, I ask, "How can you dance so good?" I sign the words as I speak. I spent the whole day practising.

She takes out a pad and writes, "I feel vibrations."

"You feel vibrations?"

She nods.

"That's why the speakers were turned to the floor?"

She nods again.

"You could be a professional," I say.

Rosemarie shakes her head violently, definitely negating this idea. Obviously, it has crossed her mind.

Then I ask: "Rosemarie, were you born deaf?"

She shakes her head and then mimes wiping a sweaty forehead.

"You were sick?"

She indicates a thermometer, places it in my mouth, then removes it and discovers I have a high reading.

"A high fever?"

She nods and dots her face with her fingers.

"The measles?"

She nods again.

"Measles, huh. Jeez, everybody had measles."

She shrugs and looks out across the river. I touch her arm and she turns back. "And then you just lost your hearing?"

She holds up six fingers.

157

"Six years old? That's when you lost it?"

She nods.

"Ahh. Boy, when I was six years old, you couldn't shut me up. Motor mouth, my mother called me, 'cause when I wasn't runnin' around singin', I was always talking."

Rosemarie signs, "Motor mouth."

I smile. "Yeah. That's my nickname. Do you have a nickname?" As I sign these words, I scratch my nose.

She looks at me puzzled. I guess she thinks it's some kind of new sign.

"No," I tell her, laughing. "I was just scratchin' my nose." I repeat the sign "nickname" without scratching.

As she starts to answer, I take her hands in mine.

"No. Tell me."

She looks up at me. Then I hit her with it.

"Rosemarie, can you talk?" She gets up and walks away.

I hit the nerve. I move to her side as thunder rips through the sky and it begins to drizzle.

I turn her around and look right into her eyes, cupping her face with my hands.

"Rosemarie. Just say my name." I knew the minute she got up from the swing that she could talk. It's her voice she's ashamed of. "Just say my name," I say, leaning in and turning my ear toward her mouth.

After a long pause I hear:

"Drew."

I feel a chill. Her voice *is* different. It's high, it's light, it's very airy, There's no bass to it. Because, as I learn later, when a person's deaf, they don't speak from their abdomen like we do. We speak from the pit of our stomachs, that's where our voices come from. But a deaf person, since he can't hear himself, has to speak from his throat, and therefore his voice is high.

Looking at Rosemarie, you'd never know she's deaf, like I didn't. But hearing her, you know right away she's different.

As the rain pours down, I kiss her. I don't give a damn about her voice. What I care about is her. And she knows it, 'cause she's kissing me back.

We're getting drenched, but were not letting go of each other.

A two-tone Lincoln Continental pulls up alongside the park. I look over as Pinky climbs out from behind the wheel, followed by Johnny. Just what I don't need now! Pinky struts into the park. The taps on his heels scrape against the night.

"You slapped my brother around. You think I forget that?" Pinky says as he comes forward, taking a stance, Johnny by his side.

I position myself protectively in front of Rosemarie.

"'Cause I didn't say anything at the club, you think I'd let you get away with smacking around my family? Who's this fetching lovely?" he says, sweeping his eyes over Rosemarie. I want to punch him out, but I stay cool.

I take Rosemarie's hand. "Good night, Pinky," I say, leading Rosemarie away. He blocks my path.

"Your brother plays, your brother pays, a dollar a day!"

I look Johnny right in the eye. "Remember what I told you would happen if you ever lay a hand on my brother again."

Pinky flares up.

"Don't talk to him! You wanna threaten somebody, threaten me!"

"The same goes for you!" I say, and start to walk around him. He exposes a pistol tucked in his belt. Thunder rips through the sky and lightning flashes over our heads as he grins. Johnny spits and snarls.

"Let's get some money," Johnny says, turning to Pinky. "You said we'd get some money."

Pinky turns to me. "You smashed the door to his clubhouse, we'll let you pay for that now." Johnny grabs for Rosemarie's pocketbook. I whirl around and level Johnny with a right hook. Pinky whips out the gun.

For the longest moment we just stare at each other. Rosemarie is squeezing my hand, scared. But I'm not scared. I know Pinky won't use it. As a matter of fact I'm sure it's not even loaded. He's had that six-shot Saturday-night special since high school. He bought it from a hood named Arnie who stayed back twice and, though Pinky's always pictured himself becoming an important, respected New Jersey crime figure, he'll never amount to anything. I take Rosemarie's hand and lead her away fast.

Pinky yells, "I'm telling you—stop!"

It's pouring now as I lead Rosemarie out of the park.

"Shoot!" I hear Johnny scream at Pinky. Rosemarie and I cross the street as Johnny yells.

"Why didn't you shoot?"

"Who told you to grab the pocketbook?" Pinky growls.

"You're scared of them," Johnny snarls and Pinky smacks Johnny across the face.

"I'm scared of nobody!"

"You're scared of him and he's always been tougher than you."

"Shut up," Pinky screams. "I'll shoot you!"

"You had the gun and you're still scared," Johnny whines.

"Where are you going?" Pinky says.

Johnny abandons all respect for his older brother and walks away. He mutters as he goes . . .

"My brother's a coward."

Pinky spins around as Rosemarie and me disappear around a corner. Shame and self-hatred infect every pore of his small-time, never-going-anywhere punk's body.

"Drew!"

After a good distance away, I pause in an alleyway. Rosemarie is shivering and she's scared. I stroke her wet hair and try to relax her.

"You okay?"

She nods.

"Bet I didn't tell you how pretty you look when you're scared. Really."

I pick her chin up with my hand and look into her eyes.

"He won't do anything. He's just a lot of hot air." We hear Pinky screech away in his Lincoln Continental.

"Some people," I tell Rosemarie, "just live on hate. There, he's gone." I lean down and kiss her again. We're getting soaked but it doesn't matter.

As another bolt of lightning races across the sky, Rosemarie lifts her face to the rain and lets the water cascade over her skin.

"Tears from 'eaven—God is crying," she says. Some sounds she has trouble pronouncing. H's and P's especially. I cup her face with my hands.

"But not for us . . ." I say.

She looks up at me. I take her hand and a funny sensation ripples through my body. I feel strong. Taller. Happy and proud is what I'm feeling as I walk through the rain with Rosemarie Lemon at my side.

We have no place to go but my apartment. I'm praying everybody's asleep. We walk down the hall to the door as I take the keys from my pocket.

"I'm getting my own place soon," I tell her as a small puddle forms around our feet.

As I unlock the door I mumble to myself, "I gotta get my own place."

We step inside and I can hear the TV. You have to go through the kitchen to get to the living room, and the kitchen is a wreck. Somehow it looks even worse than it usually does.

I watch Rosemarie as she looks around. Unwashed dishes are piled in the sink. An empty frozen turkey dinner tray spills out of the garbage.

"The maid called in sick today."

She smiles.

I tell her I'll be right back, and go down to my room to get my robe out of my closet. Raymond is asleep, and believe me, I don't make a sound. As a matter of fact, I hold my breath the entire time I'm in the room.

I tiptoe back down the hall and into the kitchen, where I hand Rosemarie the robe and pull aside the curtain which separates the living room from the kitchen.

Nathan is snoring on the couch. His checkerboard—he plays checkers with himself—is on the coffee table and the sign-off pattern is revolving on the TV set.

I turn to Rosemarie and gesture toward the snoring fat man.

"My grandfather."

She nods and I wake him up.

"Wha . . . wha . . ." he grunts, and eventually focuses on Rosemarie.

"Is that her?" he mumbles, sitting up fast.

"Yeah," I nod. I try to get the introductions out of the way as fast as possible.

"This is my grandfather, Nathan. This is Rosemarie."

He pulls on his glasses, and his face becomes alarmed.

"You're soaking wet. The girl is shivering!"

"I'm okay," Rosemarie says in her voice which is really not bad at all.

"You do talk!" Nathan exclaims.

"Talks, walks, eats. She does everything. Even gets wet."

I help him to his feet.

"Where are you going?" he asks me, still looking at Rosemarie.

I smile at Rosemarie, "He's still asleep."

"I'm awake," he says. "I want to talk to Rosemarie after she's dry."

"Some other time. Let's go."

"After she's dry," he says again.

"Some other time," I say firmly, and now I physically escort him out of the living room, closing the curtain behind me.

I lead him down the corridor into Frank's empty room and sit him on the bed.

"Stay here and go to sleep."

"Frank took Helen to the movies."

"Yeah, I know. Now good night and don't come out."

"Beautiful girl," Nathan smiles.

I nod and close the door behind me. I go back into my room, tiptoeing again ever so gently. Step up to my dresser, and slowly remove a T-shirt from the top drawer. Raymond tosses in his sleep.

I freeze.

Then go over to a closet, remove a pair of dungarees from the shelf, and being as quiet as possible, I sneak out of the room, closing the door behind me. I go into the bathroom to change.

After quickly rubbing a towel through my hair, I pad down the hallway back through the kitchen and up to the curtain.

I realize there's no way I can know if she's already changed. I knock on the wall, which makes me feel like a genius again.

I pull the curtain aside a little bit and peek. She's standing there by the heater wrapped up in my robe, her dress draped over a wooden chair.

I enter, and she turns.

I just stare at her, soaking up how good she looks. She smiles tantalizingly. The room is only lit by a soft hue from a street light. I move to her. Gently, I take her in my arms.

As we kiss, her fingers bury themselves in my damp hair. My arms circle her waist. I cover her mouth with mine.

Our kiss goes on and on . . . We gravitate to the couch and slide down, her body melting into mine. I slip my hand inside her robe and caress her breast. She breathes hot into my mouth . . .

Raymond, meanwhile, is coming down the hallway in his T-shirt and jockey shorts. He enters the kitchen, opens the refrigerator, grabs a carton of milk and gulps thirstily. The light from the refrigerator brings out a lonely cockroach from under a floorboard. It crawls on Raymond's toe.

"*Ahhh!*"

He leaps back and drops the bottle of milk. It crashes to the floor. I look at Rosemarie.

"Don't move. I'll be right back."

I pull the curtain aside and poke my head in.

Raymond's staring at the pool of milk surrounding his toes.

"What are you doing?"

He whirls around, "Jeez, you scared me!"

"What the hell you doin'?"

"A cockroach attacked my big toe."

"Clean it up and get back to bed," I tell him, unamused. All of a sudden his face lights up as he realizes: "Somebody in there with you?"

"I'm just watchin' TV."

He gets excited.

"Lemme see her!"

"Go back to bed, Raymond!"

He leans forward and whispers. "You gettin' anything?"

I duck my head back inside the living room and then I hear: "I'm comin' in!"

I stick my head back into the kitchen and snarl, "You do and I'll kill you."

"Does she have a little sister? Ask her. C'mon, Drew, I'm fifteen. I'm goin' through puberty!"

Rosemarie pulls the curtain aside. I sigh, extremely frustrated. Raymond lights up at the sight of her. He looks at me.

"We just got wet and the clothes are dryin'."

His face bursts into a grin.

"Take that stupid look off your face."

"I'm not stupid. I'm Raymond."

"She knows who you are."

Rosemarie smiles, "Hi, Raymond."

"Wow—you don't sound bad! You sound foreign!"

I glare at my brother but Rosemarie places a hand on my shoulder, telling me it's all right. I hear a cough and footsteps. Nathan arrives and flicks on the kitchen light.

"Aw, Christ," I exclaim.

"What's goin' on?" he says, looking at Rosemarie. "You dry?"

Boom!

A thud is heard outside the hallway.

"Somebody!" Helen's voice calls.

I open the door. Helen's trying to lug my old man to the door. Both of them are drenched and Frank is stone drunk. Also, I notice there are now blond streaks in Helen's hair.

"Oh my God, look at this!" I mutter.

Helen's fuming. "We went to Ernie's bar after the movie. Frank got into a drinking match with Ernie!"

"A three-ring circus." I sigh.

I get out and pull my father's arm around my shoulder and carry him inside. He lifts his head and peers at Rosemarie through bloodshot eyes.

"Ya must be dream girl." he garbles.

"Hold still," I tell him and sling him over

167

my shoulder in a fireman's carry. Rosemarie clutches at the robe, very embarrassed. Helen tries to make her feel all right.

"It's okay. You got wet, right? I'm Helen. He's drunk. No need to explain anything in this house!"

I travel down the hallway with Frank over my shoulder, push open his door with my foot and dump him down on his bed. Helen comes in behind me, and then starts to undress him.

I head back to the kitchen. Rosemarie's helping Raymond clean up the milk.

Nathan pulls me aside. His unshaven face is a portrait of seriousness.

"This is a nice girl," he says.

Meanwhile, Helen is looking around my father's room, which she's never been in before. When they stay together it's always at her place. My father giggles as she peels off his wet socks.

"It tickles."

She tickles him.

"Stop it."

She laughs and tickles him more.

"Stop it, you're killin' me!"

He laughs like a little baby and pulls his foot away. Helen slides down by his side and kisses his neck, feeling sexy.

My father turns around, looks at her, then suddenly gets off the bed and moves to the corner.

"C'mere."

"Where you goin'," she coos. "C'mon back."

"C'mon over here," my father grunts un-romantically.

She doesn't understand.

"Frank? Standing up?"

"Off the bed. Come over here."

She looks at him.

"I want you off the bed." He turns away.

She still doesn't understand. But then her eye is caught by my father's fourteen-carat gold-framed wedding photo on the night table. She looks at my mother with her long blond hair, and then sees herself in the mirror with her blond streaks.

Suddenly it sinks in and she climbs off the bed . . .

My father mutters, "It's just . . ."

"Forget it."

He doesn't want her on the bed. No other woman's shared that bed with him.

"Let's go back to your place."

She grabs her coat.

"Where you goin'?"

I hear my father yell as Helen comes down the hallway and pulls open the front door.

"Gone . . ." She says as she leaves. And I get a feeling it's all over between him and Helen.

CHAPTER NINETEEN

THE SUN'S RISING AS I WALK ROSEMARIE TO HER door. After Helen left, we didn't hang around. The rain had let up and we just walked around for the rest of the night. She turns to me and signs as she speaks.

"I like your family."

I smile and make sure I speak slowly.

"You gotta strange sense of humor."

"I mean it, I do. Especially Raymond." Her voice really doesn't sound bad at all. I'm starting to get used to it.

"He's all right," I say.

She smiles.

"I love how you're all so close."

"We're not close, we just live together."

She smiles and I notice Mrs. Lemon is

staring out the kitchen window, watching us. I don't say anything, and kiss Rosemarie good night. Rather, I kiss her good morning.

We make plans to see each other tomorrow and I walk away humming . . .

About ten blocks later, I realize I've never heard the melody I'm humming before. It's an original. I quicken my pace. I take a left on Garden Street, instead of a right. I start to trot, heading toward the train station. I don't want to lose this melody, I want to get to the Record-Your-Own-Voice booth and lay it down before I forget it. I gotta get another tape recorder too! I gotta get another tape recorder . . .

CHAPTER TWENTY

I RECORD THE NEW MELODY AND THEN GO OVER TO buy the morning paper from Valerie. I open it up to the classified section and check the apartments for rent. There's one on Third Street. A one-bedroom, unfurnished...

When I was born my parents were living in a one-bedroom apartment. Of course I don't remember it well because I was only about three when we moved to a bigger one, but my father showed me pictures. God, what a beautiful place. He paid thirty-nine dollars a month rent and the place was huge, I mean really beautiful. High ceilings, natural wood floors, windows everywhere, sunlight pouring in from every angle. It was really a gorgeous place. My mother loved plants, so we had plants everywhere. It was too bad they tore it down to build the YMCA which sixteen years later was torched to the ground by an arsonist who was never caught.

"C'mon, you're dropping it!" I yell at Raymond. We're struggling up a narrow stairwell with an old couch.

"What'd Dad say when you told him?" Raymond asks. We finally mount the last step to the fourth floor walk-up I rented.

"I didn't. C'mon, lift your end!"

The two of us resemble Laurel and Hardy as we bonk our way down the hallway with the heavy sofa.

"Think it's long enough for you both to curl up on?" Raymond asks with a sly grin on his face.

"Don't be cute."

"That's why you're movin,' isn't it?"

"I'm movin' 'cause I'm gonna be thirty."

We finally get the couch into my new, barren, one-bedroom apartment. My clothes and possessions are everywhere—hanging on door knobs and slung over the kitchen counter, where Ricco, the Italian landlord, is waiting in a baggy undershirt. We set the couch down and I go over to Ricco as Raymond wanders around checking the place out.

"Where'd you get that?" Ricco asks, eyeing the couch.

"Goodwill," I shrug. "Look—I don't have any furniture. It'll have to do for a while—you got my key, Mister Ricco?"

"You got security?" he says, taking a bite of a bruised banana.

"Ya mean, like a-watchdog?"

"I told you. Bring a month's security." He swallows and coughs.

"I couldn't getta dog."

"A dog?"

"Yeah, but I got a baseball bat," I say holding back a grin. Ricco's got no sense of humor.

"C'mon! Security! Money! Last month's rent! First and last! It's always that way!"

I look around the empty room. He never said anything about security.

"Security for what?"

"In case you pick up in the middle of the night an' move away."

"An' take what? The Murphy bed?" It's the one piece of furniture that comes included in the rent.

"Look. I'm not gonna argue with you," he says, flinging the rotted banana in a trash barrel. "That's the way it is." He heads for the door. I stop him.

"I don't have any more! That hundred and a half cleaned me out. But I told you I got a job. I'll give ya security next week, alright? How's that?"

Ricco shakes his head, "No security, no key." He returns the hundred and fifty dollars I gave him.

"What about this?" Raymond says. He removes his gold watch and hands it to Ricco.

175

The landlord examines it. "This is an expensive watch," he says sarcastically.

"You think I'd wear junk?" Raymond snaps. "I'm his brother. He's gonna be a famous singer! This joint'll be a landmark one day!" he says, running his hand through his uncombed hair.

Ricco hands the watch back to Raymond. Raymond doesn't take it.

"What? It's solid gold!"

Ricco scrapes the watch against the door latch. The gold flakes off, exposing metal.

"Watch ain't worth five dollars." He hands the watch back to Raymond and turns to me.

"No security, no key."

I feel the heat in the back of my neck. I grab him in the hallway.

"Why didn't you tell me before I dragged all this stuff up?"

"Look man, I don't want any trouble."

"You already got trouble. What am I supposed to do with all this stuff?"

A tenant down the hallway opens his door to see what the commotion's about.

"Trouble, Mr. Ricco?" he asks, eyeing me icily.

Raymond lays a hand on my shoulder.

"Better let 'im go, Drew."

I glare at the little fat man but let him go. He smoothes the wrinkles in his undershirt, trots down the hallway and descends the steps.

I turn and stare at all the stuff me and Raymond dragged up four flights of stairs.

Raymond's contemplating his "gold" watch . . .

Raymond goes over to Demetrius's house and I drive home in low spirits. It took two hours for us to load all the stuff back into the cleaning van. I just left the couch there. . . .

Later, me and the band are over at the disco. It's all finished. It's really lavish. The floor shines and we're on the stage, bookmarked on each side by towering speakers, rehearsing a disco number. I wish I could tell you what it feels like to sing in front of a band. It is a such a great feeling. And when me and the band are really cooking, it's a feeling I can't describe in words, except that it's definitely a sexual experience. It's a high—a real, natural high. Sometimes after a song, when we've really cooked, especially if it's one of the numbers I wrote, I feel dizzy, light-headed, like I'm floating on air. My heart beats a mile a minute, and I'm aware of every muscle and organ in my body. I saw this movie a coupla months ago, called "Pumping Iron," all about body builders, Mr. Universes and Mr. Olympias, and the guy who is the king of all of them, Arnold Schwarzenegger, was describing how he felt finishing up a heavy workout. He said he felt like his whole body was having an orgasm. Sounds crazy but I understand it. Maybe an actor feels like that when he takes a bow after a great performance. Maybe a writer feels like that when he finishes reading a book he wrote. And a dancer after a dance, and a painter after he finishes a canvas—. Maybe I'm wrong, but I do understand it, 'cause sometimes after singing I've felt that way.

As a matter of fact, I'm feeling that way right now, as the band finishes a disco number. It was great . . . Believe me, we never sounded better.

Mr. Patterson walks across the floor carrying a portable radio, looking like a proud father. We stop playing as he looks up to us.

Patterson checks his watch and turns on the portable radio. "Listen," he says. A song ends and we hear Devilish Dan, a local deejay.

"Devilish Dan here! I want to remind you all about the grand opening of Patterson's Landmark! A brand-new disco featuring live music and dancing to the sounds of Hoboken's own—The New Jersey Turnpike, featuring the voice of Drew Rothman! Remember everybody—that's Saturday night! This Saturday night! I'll see you there, I'll be there! This Saturday night." Mr. Patterson turns the radio off. I'm grinning. Me and the band exchange looks.

Petey twirls a drumstick in his left hand.

"Sounds good. Got a great ring to it. Good commercial."

"How does it feel up there?" Patterson asks.

I look out over the huge dance floor and answer into the live microphone. "Powerful."

"All right, let's hear another song." I turn to Petey and he starts drumming. Mark, my guitarist, joins in next. Gino starts on the piano and Fred picks up on his sax. We break into a new song, it's called "Disco Lady," and as I start to rock out I notice Pinky by the bar, glaring at me.

After rehearsal we all go out and have a few beers, and then I climb into my van and head for home. I park in front of my building and enter. I trudge up the three flights of steps, whistling, feeling good. I had forgotten all about Ricco's apartment.

She's waiting by the door, Mrs. Lemon is.

"Oh . . . hello," I say, surprised. She looks strange and very out of place standing in front of my door.

She doesn't say anything, just looks at me. I unlock the door and clear my throat, nervous. She's just staring at me.

"Do you, uh, want to come in?"

She nods. I open the door and step aside. She enters.

The apartment is in its usual disarray. Someone even left the refrigerator door open.

Mrs. Lemon surveys the mess and looks at me. I close the refrigerator, then point toward the living room. Clothes are strewn everywhere. I remove a pair of Nathan's pants from the couch and Mrs. Lemon sits.

"Do you, uh, want somethin' to drink? Juice, milk, ice water or somethin', Mrs. Lemon?"

She shakes her head, then notices a racing form on the coffee table.

"Mrs. Lemon, I'm . . . I'm very serious about your daughter."

She feels something underneath her. She reaches under her skirt and pulls out one of Nathan's checkers.

She looks up at me as she places the checker on the coffee table.

"Drew," she says nicely, "have you ever sat down and thought what it would be like to be married to a deaf person?"

"As a matter of fact, I was thinkin' about that just as I was comin' home . . . because I got a job. It's gonna pay well, and I'd like to take Rosemarie to see some doctors."

Mrs. Lemon turns away and shakes her head. This makes me angry. She reminds me of an English teacher I had in high school who always tried to make me feel stupid because I never could get the hang of diagramming sentences. Prepositions always screwed me up.

"I'm talkin' about specialists, Mrs. Lemon!"

She turns back, her face hard, but then she softens somewhat and replies quietly, "Rosemarie is deaf! Permanently and profoundly deaf. No doctor on earth could bring back her hearing."

"Are you sure?" I ask and then brighten up. "They're inventing cures for everything these days."

Mrs. Lemon has to fight back emotion.

"Her hearing cells are permanently damaged, Drew. Rosemarie will go to her grave never hearing another sound. She'll never hear you sing."

I have to hide it. To tell the truth, I'm

shocked. Sometimes I don't think things out. I assumed there could always be an operation.

She continues in a not unfriendly tone. Suddenly as I'm looking at her, all I see is a concerned mother. A lonely woman who feels more than a little guilt over her only daughter's condition. A mother alone, with no man in her life, wanting the best for her daughter and afraid that daughter may make a wrong choice and be hurt.

"You'll never be able to turn to Rosemarie and say, 'How did that sound, honey?' You'll never be able to talk to her in the dark. You'll never be able to talk to her on the phone. Your whole life will change drastically. These things may not sound like much now, but if you do start to make it and I wish you luck"—she means it—"if you do, what happens then?"

I think it over for a moment . . .

"What I know is what I feel now."

"Drew," she says, "a year from now you could walk away from Rosemarie. There'll be a hundred girls for you out there . . . But know this, for a deaf girl the pickings are slim. Scott, the other deaf teacher in the school, who Rosemarie has been seeing up until she met you—he loves her. He wants to marry her."

I'm surprised but I don't say anything.

"Didn't know that, did you? She was going to say yes, until she met you. Do me a favor, will you? Think it over . . . Then think it over again . . ."

She stands, brushes off her skirt and lets herself out without another word.

I sit there, alone in the apartment, lost in the reality of what I've heard.

After a moment I walk over to the old upright piano in the corner of the living room. . . . I sit on the bench for a moment in a kind of daze and start plunking the opening chords to the song I started to write the other day in the booth.

CHAPTER TWENTY-ONE

THAT NIGHT ROSEMARIE AND I TAKE A WALK DOWN to an abandoned pier not far from the train station. We walk out to a ferry slip that's no longer in use and hasn't been for ten years. We lean against the railing, sipping hot chocolate from styrofoam cups. Somehow I get into talking about my family.

"I was just about to move out when my mother died. I decided to stay home and try to hold things together. I don't think I've done such a good job . . ." I take a long sip of hot chocolate and look at her.

She has her hair pulled back in a bun. I like it that way.

"I talked to your mother today."

She's surprised, a little angry.

"What did she say?"

"She said you'll never be able to hear my music."

She looks up at me ...

"I won't ..."

I pull her into my arms and kiss her. I want her to know it isn't gonna matter to me. All I know is what I feel now, is what I told her mother. I pour my feelings through my lips as they melt into hers. Rosemarie responds by pressing her body hard against mine. She's three inches shorter than me and fits perfectly ... I feel so hot. Our tongues are dueling.

I gotta make love to her.

I pull back and look at her. Her face is flushed and warm. She looks into my eyes and it's a mutual decision. Actually, it's a need. An urgent need.

I take her hand. We head back toward the van, fast. We can't keep our hands off each other.

We climb up the four flights and down the hallway to the apartment Ricco wouldn't rent to me. I slip a penknife into the lock and quietly jimmy it open. The apartment is dark and empty. I turn to Rosemarie and nod. She steps inside and I quietly close the door behind us and chain-lock it. As I turn around she kisses me. My heart is pounding and I want this night to last a year. I take her hand and lead her into the bedroom. I pull a candle out of my pocket and she lights it.

As I pull down the Murphy bed, she

walks over to the window and stares outside at the street . . .

I come up behind her and slip my arms around her waist. She turns, and then our mouths merge and so do our bodies.

We drift over to the bed and down onto it. I unbutton her blouse. She opens my shirt. I undress her . . . then she helps me undress myself. I lean her back on the bed and we can see the shadows of our naked bodies on the wall.

Using the shadow, she signs three words: "I want you."

I draw her down onto my body. She's . . . she's so warm. Her breasts feel so great against my chest. I caress the back of her neck with my left hand as my right hand travels down her soft backside and over her thighs . . . Gently I push her over and roll on top of her. We kiss and touch and then she rolls back on top of me and kisses me down my neck to my chest . . . I'm quivering in every pore of my body. It feels like there's a soft current of electricity running through me.

After a few moments of ecstacy, I pull her face up to mine . . . I start there and cover her whole body with kisses. Never in my whole life have I felt so great in giving. Never.

And after . . .

After is amazing, too. See, a lotta times after I've been with someone, well, after we're finished I want to leave or go to sleep. I don't want to hang around. I don't want to make believe I really care when I don't. That's why a few months ago, I just stopped dating. I just couldn't fill up a night with somebody I didn't care about. Maybe this sounds hard, but I'd just decided I'd rather be alone.

But now, sitting up in the Murphy bed with Rosemarie asleep with her head resting on my chest, I don't want this moment to stop. I want to freeze it and hold it as I'm holding her. My left arm is asleep because she's lying across me at an angle, but I'm not gonna budge it 'cause I don't want to wake her. She looks so great. She's glowing.

The words come out unconsciously as I stroke her hair.

"I love you, Rosemarie."

Hearing myself say what I feel is a revelation. Sometimes a person says something he doesn't know he knows until he hears himself say it. Now, I know it.

I love this woman.

My mind drifts off and I start thinking about a life with Rosemarie, not aware Rosemarie is awake and looking up at me. She is staring at my eyes which are looking into the future, thinking about us . . . about a family which I'm dying to have. After all, I'm turning thirty. When my son is twenty, I'll be fifty. That's a big enough gap as it is.

"Was it good?" she asks.

I look at her a moment . . .

This time I make sure she sees my lips.

"Rosemarie . . . I love you."

CHAPTER TWENTY-TWO

FRANK IS BEHIND THE COUNTER WAITING ON MRS. Capucci, a hefty Italian woman with a large mole on her nose. Raymond's just hanging around, bored, smacking the gumball machine.

Mrs. Capucci stares with a shocked look on her face at the blouse that Frank burned a hole in. But now the blouse has two holes. One on each shoulder. Two little holes with pink stitching on the inside of each hole.

"You see, Mrs. Capucci," my father tries to explain "what happened was . . . Raymond stop it!" Raymond is still smacking the gumball machine.

The phone rings. Frank says, " 'Scuse me a minute," and after hearing who is on the line, moves as far away as he can for privacy.

Raymond meanders over to Mrs. Capucci who is muttering. "My favorite blouse," she says to herself.

"No, no, no, Mrs. Capucci," Raymond says as he comes around the counter, "this is the latest style from New York City. The vent shoulder look. Very sexy. This is gonna look beautiful on. Wait till you get home and put it on for Mr. Capucci. You'll be the first woman in Hoboken with this look. You'll be a trend-setter."

"Trend-setter," she sighs sarcastically. Her eyes scan the room and find me, sitting in a corner reading the *Star Ledger*.

"Look at this, Drew! My favorite blouse! What're you gonna do about it?"

"I'm sorry, Mrs. Capucci. It was an accident. We tried to make it look good."

"It doesn't look good!"

I bang open the cash register and pull out a ten dollar bill.

"Will this be okay?"

She takes it and shoots Raymond an angry look.

"Trend-setter!"

After Mrs. Capucci leaves, I turn to Raymond.

"Go to school."

He pulls out a deck of cards, and like a pro, fans them with one hand.

"Pick a card."

I grab the deck away and usher him out the door. My father, meanwhile, is having a very serious conversation with his bookie on the phone. I can't hear everything he says, but he seems very upset. His last words are "Don't worry, I swear! Yeah! Yeah! I'll talk to you very soon . . ."

I got to ask my old man about Rosemarie. "You got a minute? I want to talk to you about something."

"Not now," he says. He yells back at Nathan who's on the sewing machine. "Be back later," he says, grabs his coat and hurries out the door.

Frustrated, I wander to the back of the store where Nathan is.

"You gotta minute?"

He looks at me.

"I got millions of minutes. What's up?"

I start to fidget with the silver dollar, twirling it over knuckles like one of those Vans did . . .

"Nate . . . I really dig this girl."

"So?"

"Nah, you don't understand."

"I understand."

I stop pacing and look at him. He's nodding. He does understand.

"Yeah, I know you do. Nate . . . the last few days we've been spending a lot of time together. Little things happened, y'know, not big things, but little things that make me realize how many miles of difference there is between us."

"Yes," Nathan says, biting the thread off a zipper he's just sewed into a skirt . . .

I flip the coin, catch it between two knuckles and continue.

"If I'm not lookin' at her when I'm talkin' . . . If she doesn't see what I'm sayin', it sounds funny, but if she doesn't see what I'm sayin' . . . she doesn't hear me."

Nathan shrugs, "You gotta learn to look at her when you talk."

"It's not that simple."

"Nothin' worthwhile comes easy."

I spin the silver dollar next to his sewing machine.

"I dunno . . . I just don't know . . . maybe she'd be better off with this other guy."

"Don't," Nathan says, as he stops the spinning coin.

I look at him.

"Don't think—just go by your feelings . . . Look, you finally have the relationship you've been wanting and waiting for—. Sure it's gonna take work. She's not the fantasy girl you always thought she'd be. But real never is easy."

CHAPTER TWENTY-THREE

I GO OVER TO PATTERSON'S, PICK UP THE POSTER advertising the opening of the club, and drive straight to Rosemarie's school.

As I travel down the hallway I hear music blaring from the gym. I open the door and Rosemarie, looking terrific in leotards, is dancing alone. I watch, unnoticed, until she spots me. She smiles, embarrassed.

"No, don't stop! Go on, keep goin'!" But the record's over.

She dances over. I kiss her, then show her the poster. Rosemarie grins and takes it.

"Mine?"

I nod. "And that's not all." I pull the *Star Ledger* out of my back pocket and open it to the entertainment section. There is an ad which reads:

THE PAUL JANSSEN DANCE COMPANY
TO AUDITION REPLACEMENTS FOR
THE COMING SEASON

She looks up at me. She shakes her head.

"Why not? It's what you want."

"No I don't," she says and turns away.

I walk around in front of her, "There's nothing to be afraid of, it's just an audition."

"I don't want to audition. I'm a teacher," she says, her hands signing angrily.

"A school teacher who dreams of dancing."

"It's a nice poster," she says.

"There's nothing to be afraid of. It's just an audition!"

"Drew!"

"Why not?"

"You're making me angry!"

"Good! Get angry, but try. You've got to try. You'll never know if you don't try."

"I don't want to know!" she says and moves away. Suddenly she turns.

"I'm deaf, don't you understand? I can't hear music."

"But you feel vibrations."

"It won't work! There are no deaf dancers in 'earing companies. Maybe I could get in a deaf company but I could never get into a 'earing company."

"You don't know that for sure."

"It's impossible!"

"Great. If everybody thinks it's impossible, you won't have any competition!"

"Oh, Drew."

"Oh, Rosemarie . . . Rosemarie, look at me."

I put my hands on her shoulders and look right into her eyes. "I started out as a joke . . ."

She looks at me questioningly.

"Yeah, I was breaking my back every night in the brewery, dreamin' of becoming a singer, so I said to myself, 'Am I goin' to die a dreamer?' Like my mother who always wanted to be an actress and my father talked her out of it. Or my father who always wanted to live in California but my grandfather talked *him* out of it. Everybody's always talkin' everybody else outta trying to do what they want to do . . . and it's easy for people to get talked out of it 'cause people are afraid to want something 'cause they might not get it. Rosemarie, I say be a dancer if that's what you want. At least try. Take the chance. Take the gamble. The worst that can happen is they'll say no, but you've got to try." Rosemarie is staring at me, wide-eyed. I think I'm getting through to her.

"I saw you dance and I know you're terrific. Yeah, you are terrific!"

She smiles.

"You do want to be a dancer, don't you? You do, don't you?"

She admits a lifelong dream.

"I always have," she says.

"Well, you could do it! I'll come with you! I'll be there! I'll be right by your side!"

There's a sparkle in her eyes and at that moment I know that she *is* going to try. I put my arms around her waist, and look directly into her eyes. I say something I've never said to anyone else in the world.

"Rosemarie . . . I believe in you."

CHAPTER TWENTY-FOUR

I'M ON MY WAY TO MEET ROSEMARIE FOR LUNCH. As I amble down the sidewalk, I run into Korina.

"Korina, how are you?"

She comes up to me, smiling.

"I haven't seen you in a while. Have you met the princess?" she asks. I can see in her eyes she's hoping I haven't.

"Yeah," I nod as she flips her long hair back with her left hand. "Everything you said was right. You're always right, Korina. Your cards are always right."

She forces a smile and takes my hand between hers. "And is she special? She is, isn't she?"

I nod.

"I'm really happy for you." She presses

my hand. "I'm really happy for you. It's not good to be alone."

I really don't know what to say to her and I'm feeling a little awkward because she's holding my hand.

"Thanks."

"A kiss for good luck." She raises herself up on her toes and kisses me on the lips. As luck would have it, Rosemarie is just then coming around the corner. She sees the kiss and the sight makes her cold inside. She can't believe it. I turn and catch sight of her but before I can say anything she turns and heads back around the corner. Quickly I excuse myself from Korina and trot after her.

I round the corner but she's nowhere in sight. I keep going down the street and miss her. At that moment, Pinky steps up to Rosemarie. He backs her up against a brick wall with a twisted look on his face and a staple gun in his hand. Pinky's been putting up the band's poster, and naturally he's in an angry mood. I saw one poster, it had ten staples over my face.

"Remember me? Don't be scared. Pinky's not going to hurt you. Hey, nice body! What's your name?"

Rosemarie backs up and bumps into a garbage can. Pinky dumps his armful of posters into it. A stray cat screams and darts across the alley.

"Answer me," Pinky says, pressing. Rosemarie can't understand what he's saying. "Am I talking too fast?"

Pinky leans in and breathes out. "What's wrong with your voice?"

"I can't 'ear."

"Sure you got ears!"

"I'm deaf," Rosemarie says. Pinky is surprised. He studies Rosemarie, his mood becoming more and more eerie.

"Really?" Pinky asks. Rosemarie nods, scared.

"Please let me go." she says. Pinky runs the staple gun up her arm.

"Deaf, Jesus," he says. Rosemarie's shivering, she's scared. Pinky's getting a thrill out of frightening her.

"Your boyfriend thinks he's really hot, don't he?" She doesn't answer. He leans in, breathing on her face.

"He's nothin', ya hear me, nothing!!"

Rosemarie pushes him off. He grabs at her, catching her blouse and ripping it. She screams.

"*Drew!*"

I fly down the street toward her. Pinky's in the alleyway. He shakes her, trying to shut her up.

"Shut up!"

Rosemarie clutches her blouse trying to cover herself and fend him off. He spins around in the alley. He whips out the gun that's tucked in his belt as I dart into the opening. Like a rabid dog he growls as he holds Rosemarie with his arm across her throat, holding her in front of him.

I charge in and he fires! Rosemarie screams. He actually fires. A bullet rips into the pavement an inch from my foot . . . I look up at him!?

"You owe me money for wreckin' Johnny's clubhouse."

"Let her go."

"Fifty dollars. I want it now!"

His pitted face is sweating and I can see he's in a very bad way. He resembles a rubber band stretched to its limits, about to pop . . . As I speak, my voice is very, very calm.

"You want fifty dollars, Pinky? Okay . . . Let Rosemarie go, we'll go back to the cleaners and get your money."

He lifts his gun and fires into the brick wall less than a foot from my head!

"You get it. You go get it. We'll wait here! Go get it!!"

Now I am scared because Pinky *is* cracking up. I can hear windows opening across the street and people popping their heads out.

"*What's goin' on?*" a man bellows.

As Pinky looks up, I rush him. I grab the wrist holding the gun, and yank him off Rosemarie. She runs as the gun goes off twice in the air.

Pinky and I go tumbling into the garbage cans fighting for the gun. He jabs a finger in my eye and I hit him in the face with my left hand. He gets his shoe between us and kicks me off. I spring to my feet fast as he levels the gun at my face.

I freeze.

The slightest movement of his trigger finger and I'm dead.

A police siren whines in the distance as we stare at each other. Rosemarie, also frozen, watches from the opening of the alley . . .

He looks from her to me, back to her, then to me again.

He bites his trembling lip and, as the police siren gets closer I say, "Pinky, what're you doin' this for?"

"Shut up!!"

I realize he's more scared than I am. Moisture drips from his face and I can't tell if it's sweat or his eyes tearing.

Suddenly he flings the gun down and bolts out of the alley. Rosemarie runs into my arms and I hold her tight, as the police car screeches up and Ronnie and his partner spring out.

I don't know if you can understand what happened next. Rosemarie does. I've told her all about my past with Pinky and she somehow understands.

When Ronnie asks me which way Pinky went, I tell him Pinky was heading toward the train station, when actually he went the opposite way.

CHAPTER TWENTY-FIVE

IT'S BEEN THREE DAYS AND PINKY'S TOTALLY disappeared. Johnny too. Him, Pinky, the car and most of their clothes are gone. I don't think I'll ever see Pinky again. At least not for a long, long time.

That night Rosemarie and I go back to Ricco's apartment. It's now mine. Mr. Patterson gave me an advance so I was able to give the man his rent and security. Raymond and I moved all the stuff back day before yesterday.

We enter the bedroom, which now has some signs of life 'cause I brought some clothes and hung a few pictures on the walls. I give Rosemarie a present I'd bought for her. It's a little music box. You open it up and a little dancing ballerina twirls around as this melody chimes.

She grins and kisses me.

I sweep her up and carry her into the bedroom with our lips still locked. We breathe through each other's mouths. Gently I place her on the bed, and like a blanket cover her body with my body. She starts to laugh and I catch it. We break apart laughing. We can't stop. I don't even know what we're laughing about, but we can't stop. Tears come to her eyes, and I don't understand because she's still laughing with a huge grin on her face. Suddenly she hugs me, she presses her warm cheek against mine and I feel the wetness of her tears against my face.

In my ear she whispers, "I love you, Drew."

I grip her so tight I swear I wanna pull her body right into mine. We kiss and I slide my hand behind her neck. I love to hold her this way . . . one hand around her neck and one on her back side. She dips her hands under my armpits and holds my shoulders. She pushes her pelvis firmly into mine. God . . . Oh my God. Caroline and I were never this good. All the women I've been with put together were never this good. Rosemarie is a diamond, a hundred carat diamond. All at once I feel possessive. I wanna protect her. I don't want her to ever be hurt again, by anyone, for any reason.

She pulls her head back and looks at me strangely, tilts her head and looks at me questioningly. "What?" she asks.

"Huh?" I answer.

"What are you thinking?" she asks.

"Nothing," I say.

"Me too," she smiles.

I search in her eyes for what she means. She smiles and cups my face with her hands.

"I won't share you with anyone either," she whispers.

I get such a chill. How . . . How did she know . . . ?

CHAPTER TWENTY-SIX

ROSEMARIE LATER TOLD ME IT WAS THE MOST terrifying experience of her life. . . .

The dance company is holding auditions at the Stanley Theatre. Rosemarie enters through the backstage door, where a group of dancers are limbering up doing exercises, waiting for their numbers to be called to go out on stage and audition. I'm supposed to meet her there at one. She looks at her watch—it's one.

A voice calls:

"Are you here to audition? You there . . . are you here to audition?"

A dancer taps Rosemarie. "She talking to you, honey!"

Rosemarie looks over. An assistant behind a desk is saying something and holding out a

card to her. She walks over. The assistant asks
Rosemarie her name so she can put it down on
the list. She doesn't want them to hear her different voice. She doesn't want to tell them she's
deaf so she just leans down and writes her name
on the list without saying it. The assistant hands
Rosemarie a card with a number 30 on it.

"Your name, your address, your phone
number, and your availability. Next!"

Rosemarie doesn't see the woman's lips
and gets nothing. She drifts away with the card
not knowing what to write on it. Then she
notices another dancer filling the card out and
sees what they want. She fills out the card.

She looks up at the clock again.

At that moment, I'm in my apartment
with my coat on and my keys in my hand waiting
for Raymond.

"C'mon Raymond, I gotta meet Rosemarie! I'm already late!"

He yells from the bedroom as he pulls on
a shirt and stuffs a Fig Newton in his mouth.

"Relax. You're just a few minutes away."

"Good-bye," I say and head out the door
as the phone rings.

"I'm comin'! I'm comin'!" Raymond yells.
I dip back inside and grab the phone.

"Hello."

Nathan's voice comes screaming through
the receiver. He's frantically yelling something
about my father. Something about kerosene and
that I'd better get down there right away.

"I can't," I tell him. "I gotta meet Rosemarie at her audition. I'm droppin' Raymond at Demetrius's on the way."

He screams, "For the insurance. He's gonna burn the place down ! ! !"

"Whattaya talkin' about?"

"Your father is going to burn the store down for the insurance. He's splashing kerosene over everything. He bet the store, Drew! On that race he bet the whole store! Do you hear me?"

Suddenly the line goes dead. My father has yanked the phone wires out of the wall.

"Not now! *Not now!*" I explode.

Rosemarie, meanwhile, is being called out on stage to audition. The male choreographer calls out the numbers.

"Next five, thirty through thirty-four."

Five dancers hurry on stage with their cards. The choreographer yells at Rosemarie, who's been looking at the clock and wondering where I am. "C'mon thirty, you're on."

She nervously unhooks her skirt, drapes it over a chair along with her coat and walks out in her leotard.

Her heart pounds.

The stage is big and brightly lit. Paul Janssen, a thin ex-dancer in his late thirties, is sitting in the dark theatre with his legs propped up on the seat. His lead dancer sits next to him with a table in front of her. They watch as the choreographer collects the girls' cards and hands them to another assistant who travels up the aisle and hands them to Paul.

At that moment, Raymond and I are running across Elysian Park toward the cleaners. A light snow is falling and Christmas decorations are strung up over Hoboken.

"Look! Smoke!" Raymond yells as we speed out of the park toward the cleaners.

We burst inside.

Flames are spreading through the shop! Nathan has my father in a headlock and they're careening around, knocking over everything.

"Get the blanket!" I yell at Raymond, yanking the old, never-before-used extinguisher off the wall. I turn it upside down and it doesn't work. I fling it aside and grab a bedspread that was just cleaned. I beat the flames. Raymond yells: "I'll call the . . ."

"Don't call anybody!" I drop the blanket, then lunge at my old man and Nathan, separating them. Nathan runs to help Raymond. I topple to the floor on top of my father, who's trying to ignite more kerosene-soaked clothes. I grab his wrist.

"I'll kill ya if you don't let go!" he screams.

I rip the lighter from his hand, then run over to help Nathan and Raymond battle the flames. Suddenly, Nathan screams, "Raymond!"

My brother's Gladiator jacket catches fire.

"*Ahhhhh!*" Raymond screams, panicking and running from the store, tripping off the curb and falling into the street. I run out with the blanket, throw it over him and roll him around. Frank runs out more scared than Raymond. I get the flames out before they cause any damage.

My brother's alright. He's just scared. I look over at my old man with murder in my eyes.

He picks up the blanket, runs back into the cleaners to help Nathan, who has run back into the store and is beating the flaming counter. . . .

Rosemarie's eyes are glued on the choreographer as he demonstrates what he wants. Like the other four girls, Rosemarie is trying to match his movements as he does them.

"Okay, this is how it's gonna start—one up, hold, extend, two and three and four and five . . ." Rosemarie is trying to keep up with the others. ". . . six into a turn, a double turn, around . . ."

Rosemarie is now one beat behind the other girls because she has to see what they're doing before she can do it. The choreographer looks at her, impatient.

"Keep up back there, c'mon, hold. You're behind, number thirty."

Rosemarie sweats. Paul Janssen and his lead dancer are watching Rosemarie, who's now totally off. She comes out of a spin after all the other girls are already into the next move. He and his lead dancer exchange looks.

"I told you you should let me screen them first, Paul . . ."

"Yeah . . ."

The choreographer finishes his instructions: ". . . into a triple turn and, if you can, end finally with a split. Okay that's what I want."

As he heads toward the record player, one of the dancers asks another, "What was that again? After the double turn?"

"Around and hold, I think," a lithe Spanish dancer answers quickly massaging a cramp out of her instep. She turns to Rosemarie, "How many counts do we hold that extend? I didn't hear."

"C'mon, Claire," the ponytail snorts. "Don't ask her. She lost us after the second turn."

Beads of sweat cover Rosemarie's face . . .

We finally beat out what's left of the fire, which has gutted most of the inside of the store.

My father walks outside, sinks to the curb and drops his head into his hands. Nathan comes out and picks up the glass from one of his lenses that broke during the scuffle with my father.

Raymond stares at my father, very confused. His idol has crumbled before his eyes.

"Does this mean we're not gonna move to California?" he mumbles.

"What the hell you think's in California?" I ask.

He looks up, "Blondes."

"Everything you want is right here," Nathan says as he puts the glasses on and tries to focus with only his left eye.

"There's nothin' here," Raymond spits. "Ask Dad. He knows. There's nothin' here, right, Dad?"

Raymond doesn't want to believe the

truth. My father has ground the business into ashes and the family is broke. He wants to hear my father say he has an ace up his sleeve.

I have to make him see the truth. "Go on, Raymond, ask him. Ask him what he knows." I push Raymond toward my father. Today he'll grow up. "Go on, Raymond, ask him."

As he looks down, there are tears in his eyes.

"Daddy . . . ?"

My father can't even look up.

Nathan sinks down next to Frank. I think he's gonna yell in Frank's ear and then he just does the opposite . . .

He puts his arm around his son's shoulder, comforting. Understanding, forgiving. . . .

Sometimes I forget they are father and son.

The choreographer drops the needle down on the audition record and turns to the dancers. "Alright, girls, you're on."

At first, Rosemarie keeps up. She does the beginning, up, hold, extend. She counts to herself, her lips move, "Two and three and four and five." She even stays with the music which is on low.

Then she's lost, totally.

She forgets what's next. The choreographer watches her and shakes his head. Rosemarie's several steps behind all the other girls and totally off. She tries to catch up but only makes it worse. As the audition piece finishes,

Rosemarie doesn't hear and still dances . . . Paul Janssen and the lead dancer exchange bewildered looks.

Rosemarie looks up and realizes she's dancing alone. The other girls are staring at her. Everybody is staring at her. Her heart thunders.

She bolts off the stage, grabs her coat, and runs up the aisle and through the lobby.

She tries to pull on her coat, putting the wrong arm in the wrong sleeve. She leans against the wall, shaking, fighting back tears.

Just then, my van screeches up. I leap out and run inside. She tries to break away from me.

"I'm sorry. What happened?"

"I shouldn't 'ave come, I shouldn't 'ave come!"

"What happened? You didn't tell them?"

"Why did I think I could do it?"

I knew it was now or never. It's like the first time you dive off the high dive and do a belly flop. It hurts so bad but you gotta go right back and try again or you'll never do it.

"You can! You will! We're going back!"

She looks at me like I'm crazy. Maybe I even look crazy. There's ash on my face, my hair's a mess. My coat is burnt.

"You're gonna show them."

"What happened to you?" she asks, finally focusing on me.

"I'll tell you later. But I want you to go back."

"No," she says and tries to pull away from my arms, but I don't let go.

"Yes. You can't give up! I won't let you. Not without a fight. Nothing worthwhile comes easy, Rosemarie."

I push open the door to the theatre and walk down the aisle with Rosemarie by my side. The six finalists are on the stage. I see Janssen in the middle of the theatre and I know he's the head of the troupe.

"Excuse me. Hi! You Paul Janssen?"

He looks at me.

"Sorry to barge in like this. Actually I'm not 'cause I got something great to show you I think you missed. Her name is Rosemarie Lemon . . ." He interrupts me.

"Hey, fella, look—"

"Excuse me, Paul, I'm talking. My name is Drew Rothman and it's a pleasure to meet you."

"She had her chance."

"No, Paul, I really don't think so. See, Rosemarie is a real special girl and you got to audition her in a different kinda way, which I don't think you did."

The choreographer comes down from the stage. He's built well and maybe he's thinking of escorting us out. I spin around with a very dangerous gleam in my eye.

"Please, now, let's all stay friendly. Just hear me out, okay, fellas? You see Rosemarie couldn't hear what you told her because Rosemarie *can't hear*. Yes, she's deaf . . ."

I see that look in their faces. They're shocked.

"But you see it really doesn't matter. You'll see."

I turn back to the choreographer. "Now why dontcha go up there and show her what you want again. And just make sure you're lookin' at her when you talk to her. It's no big thing. Okay? Why don't you go?"

The choreographer looks at Janssen.

"Terrific," I say.

Janssen nods at him and the choreographer leads Rosemarie back up to the stage.

"I'll tell you what," I turn back to Janssen. "One more favor? Why don't you and the lady here watch from the front row? It's a much better view up there."

"We'll be fine here," he says with finality.

"No, I'd really rather have you sit up front. See, when a person can't hear, sight means a lot more to them. I think it'd be nice if Rosemarie could feel she had an audience. Okay? C'mon, all right?"

I begin to help Janssen out of his seat.

"Don't pull!"

I let go and he and his lead dancer reluctantly walk down the aisle toward the front row.

"That's it!" I smile. "Right this way. Terrific! What a view. How 'bout right here?"

As Janssen and his lead dancer patiently take seats, the choreographer starts to show Rosemarie and the finalists what he wants. This time he demonstrates his entire routine facing them. As he finishes his explanation I pull the stereo speakers all the way onto the stage.

"What are you doing now?" Janssen calls from the first row.

"One more minor adjustment." I turn one of the speakers to the floor, then nod to Rosemarie who's nervous as hell, but not scared nervous, excited nervous.

The choreographer walks over to the phonograph. As he's about to set the needle on the record I grab a trash barrel, flip it over between my knees and begin to accentuate the record's drum by pounding on top of the barrel.

This time Rosemarie keeps up with the dancers.

I've never seen such a beautiful sight in all my life. She's concentrating, she's feeling every movement with every muscle in her body and face. And though the steps aren't as precise as the others', I guarantee you no one's ever auditioned with more feeling. No one.

Ever.

I look out at Paul Janssen. He's on the edge of his seat. His lead dancer, too. The choreographer is scratching his face, watching.

She is great. You shoulda been there.

CHAPTER TWENTY-SEVEN

I'M NOT WEARING A WHITE SUIT LIKE IN MY FAN-
tasy. It's pale blue. The shirt is white. I'm not
tan but I feel great. And I'm not walking out
onto the stage of the MGM Grand Hotel, I'm
heading out toward the small stage for the grand
opening of Patterson's new disco.

People are standing shoulder to shoulder.
Patterson's promotion paid off. It's amazing what
a few radio spots can do. There's a lotta young
people here. I can tell a lot of 'em are high school
kids who got in using fake ID's. But no one
seems to care, the mood is high and there's a
lotta smiling faces. Hoboken needs a place like
this. As I adjust the microphone I realize this
place is probably gonna be a real big hit. Pat-

terson is definitely not stupid. The man knows what he's doing.

A fifty dollar a night part-time comic from Perth Amboy glides onto the stage and nods at me. He's the announcer. I'd forgotten about him. I drift back as he steps up to the mike. His voice is deep and clear, and though he makes jokes for a living, he makes no jokes tonight.

"Ladies and gentlemen," he says, "let's have a big hand for The New Jersey Turnpike, featuring the voice of Drew Rothman."

No women scream, and you wouldn't call the applause overwhelming, but the people are polite and I do get a good hand. I'm nervous as I step back up to the microphone. I've got butterflies in my stomach. I'm just about to say "hi" when suddenly I feel thirsty. I lean over and pick a glass of water off the top of my piano and take a quick hit. I look back over the crowd.

The kids are anxious to dance. They're anxious to get going. They came to boogie. I'm a singer in a dance band and that's what I'm here for, to give 'em music to boogie to.

"Hi, how's everybody feelin', all right?"

"Great, we're ready, cut loose," they yell back. I take my seat behind the piano, and notice Valerie and Tyrone in the crowd, Ronnie and Ricky, too, with their wives. My eyes glide across the room, and there's my father, Nathan, and Raymond sitting at one of the few tables in the room. Already I can tell just from a one-second look that the old man's drunk a little too much but he, Nathan and Raymond are watching me, and they're looking really proud. String

I notice in the bar, too. He smiles at me and points to his teeth, happy. My father gave 'em back to him this morning. Patterson is in the balcony, overseeing everything. I play the opening chords to a loud disco number. I didn't write the song, it's not great, but it's popular and a very danceable tune. Still, as I look out over the crowded room and start to play, I know I've come a long way from the topless bar and I've come a long way inside.

One-two-three-*hoo*. We break into the song. The sound is terrific in this room! I close my eyes and wail out. Within twenty seconds I push the stool back and play the piano standing like I've seen Elton John do. My fingers dance across the keyboard. I look over at Petey, who's grinning. Who cares if he's stoned, he sounds great. He twirls a drumstick in his left hand, smiles back and winks. It's funny, I never really liked the song we're playing that much, but tonight somehow it's terrific. Everybody is dancing. I look up and Patterson is keeping the rhythm of the song with two swizzle sticks on the balcony. As we finish the number the crowd gives us a huge ovation. Right away we launch into another fast number.

She said she'd be here around eight. It's about then now. My eyes are glued to the door as I sing. I know she's gonna come in any minute. Suddenly I get this feeling, and I'm right, the door opens and Rosemarie enters looking astounding, absolutely astounding, in a floor-length red dress with a red rose in her hair. Our eyes lock across the roomful of strangers. My face lights up with a grin and she beams back.

I can see my family craning their heads from the table to see what I'm looking at. Nathan stands up and waves Rosemarie over, but I don't think she sees him. She's walking toward me. Through the crowd, toward me. Rosemarie is right near the stage when we finish the tune. I bow and the crowd applauds.

"Ladies and gentlemen," I say, "I'd like to introduce the band to you. Petey on drums." They applaud. "Gino on bass, Mark on lead, Fred on sax, and I'm Drew." They clap and a girl with braces on her teeth whistles.

I look at Rosemarie, back to the band and back at Rosemarie. The crowd is anxious, they're waiting for another hot tune to dance to. I turn back to the band.

"Let's do, 'You'll be the Right One'."

Petey looks at me. "What'd you say, do what?"

"Let's do 'You'll be the Right One'."

"But they can't dance to that," Gino says.

"Let's do it anyway."

Petey, Mark and Gino exchange bewildered looks but they don't argue. I adjust the microphone as Gino takes my place on the piano bench and plays the opening chords of "You'll be the Right One." It's the same song I sang in the arcade, but this time it's a little different.

As he taps out the opening chords I reach down and lift Rosemarie up onto the stage. I twist the microphone to the side so I can face her while I sing.

The people on the dance floor are looking up at us, confused. This is a slow number. It's a ballad, you can't dance to this number. You remember the opening verses:

> *I don't know what you look like*
> *But I know that you're there*
> *Sometimes I feel your stare*
> *You'll be the right one ...*

> *Still livin' alone*
> *And wonderin' why*
> *Time just keeps flyin' by*
> *You'll be the right one ...*

Rosemarie backs up and puts her hands behind her back, placing her palms against the towering speakers so she can feel the song. I really didn't care how the crowd was gonna react. I didn't even think of it. This song is for Rosemarie and that's all I care about. But as I sing, and as they stand there watching me, it seems maybe they don't mind what I'm doing ... You see, because I'm also signing the lyrics to Rosemarie as I sing. I'm just about fluent in sign language now, and I'm singing the words with my hands so she can hear my song. I break into the new chorus that I wrote just for this night. It goes:

> *Oh yes, I need you ...*
> *With all of my heart*
> *And all of my soul*
> *I love you ...*

'Cause I'm not feelin' lonely
No longer alone
Come into my life·
You are the right one.

The look on Rosemarie's face as she watches me sing I'll never forget. And it's funny, because all those people standing on the dance floor who I thought might've been angry don't seem to mind. They're caught up in what's happening on the stage.

As I finish the song, Rosemarie reaches out and takes my hand between hers. We look into each other's eyes and, as the band plays on, I take her into my arms. Nothing else matters . . .

I've found the right one.

THE BEST OF THE BESTSELLERS
FROM WARNER BOOKS

MADE IN HOLLYWOOD by James Bacon (82-913, $2.25)

A friend and confidant to everybody who's anybody, 20-year veteran columnist Bacon tells the zaniest, bawdiest, funniest and most intimate stories about the real Hollywood. "It's all true, and this is one of the best, funniest, most titillating, most honest books ever written about Hollywood's greatest stars."
— Sunday Magazine

REELING by Pauline Kael (83-420, $2.95)

Rich, varied, 720 pages containing 74 brilliant pieces covering the period between 1972-75, this is the fifth collection of movie criticism by the film critic Newsday calls "the most accomplished practitioner of film criticism in America today, and possibly the most important film critic this country has ever produced."

THE MAKING OF SUPERMAN by David Michael Petrou (82-565, $2.25)

Out of today's awesome technology comes the most spectacular entertainment in the history of motion pictures. Now, go behind the scenes for a closeup of the biggest movie to come out of Hollywood in decades! Travel with the people who made SUPERMAN live! Featuring 16 pages of photographs.

ELVIS by Jerry Hopkins (81-665, $2.50)

More than 2 million copies sold! It's Elvis as he really was, from his humble beginnings to fame and fortune. It's Elvis the man and Elvis the performer, with a complete listing of his records, his films, a thorough astrological profile, and 32 pages of rare, early photographs!

EVERYTHING YOU'VE EVER WANTED
TO KNOW ABOUT EVERYTHING!

THE COMPLETE UNABRIDGED SUPER TRIVIA ENCYCLOPEDIA by Fred L. Worth (83-882, $2.95)

What was Xavier Cugat's theme song? Who said, "There's a sucker born every minute?" Who was Miss Hungary of 1936? What book was the bestseller of 1929? Here is a book that's bigger, better, and more fun than "The Book of Lists!" It's a collector's delight...a gambler's treasury ...'a crosswordnik's cache . . . a ferret's festival . . . EVERYTHING is here, in THE COMPLETE UNABRIDGED SUPER TRIVIA ENCYCLOPEDIA! 864 pages of pure entertainment, unmasking all the marvels from Batman to the Green Hornet — informative, interesting, fun, funny, provocative, and then some: a panoply of sports, movies, comics, television, radio, rock 'n' roll, you-name-it, at your fingertips. The biggest, the best, the most comprehensive trivia book ever created!